Tomb of the
Ten Thousand Dead

SELECTED FICTION WORKS BY L. RON HUBBARD

FANTASY

The Case of the Friendly Corpse

Death's Deputy

Fear

The Ghoul

The Indigestible Triton

Slaves of Sleep & The Masters of Sleep

Typewriter in the Sky

The Ultimate Adventure

SCIENCE FICTION

Battlefield Earth

The Conquest of Space

The End Is Not Yet

Final Blackout

The Kilkenny Cats

The Kingslayer

The Mission Earth Dekalogy*

Ole Doc Methuselah

To the Stars

ADVENTURE

The Hell Job series

WESTERN

Buckskin Brigades

Empty Saddles

Guns of Mark Jardine

Hot Lead Payoff

A full list of L. Ron Hubbard's
novellas and short stories is provided at the back.

*Dekalogy—a group of ten volumes

L. RON HUBBARD

Tomb of the
Ten Thousand Dead

GALAXY
PRESS

Published by
Galaxy Press, LLC
7051 Hollywood Boulevard, Suite 200
Hollywood, CA 90028

Printed in the United States of America.

ISBN-10 1-59212-335-X
ISBN-13 978-1-59212-335-3

Library of Congress Control Number: 2007903527

Contents

Stories from Pulp Fiction's Golden Age

A ND it *was* a golden age.

The 1930s and 1940s were a vibrant, seminal time for a gigantic audience of eager readers, probably the largest per capita audience of readers in American history. The magazine racks were chock-full of publications with ragged trims, garish cover art, cheap brown pulp paper, low cover prices—and the most excitement you could hold in your hands.

"Pulp" magazines, named for their rough-cut, pulpwood paper, were a vehicle for more amazing tales than Scheherazade could have told in a million and one nights. Set apart from higher-class "slick" magazines, printed on fancy glossy paper with quality artwork and superior production values, the pulps were for the "rest of us," adventure story after adventure story for people who liked to *read*. Pulp fiction authors were no-holds-barred entertainers—real storytellers. They were more interested in a thrilling plot twist, a horrific villain or a white-knuckle adventure than they were in lavish prose or convoluted metaphors.

The sheer volume of tales released during this wondrous golden age remains unmatched in any other period of literary history—hundreds of thousands of published stories in over nine hundred different magazines. Some titles lasted only an issue or two; many magazines succumbed to paper shortages during World War II, while others endured for decades yet. Pulp fiction remains as a treasure trove of stories you can read, stories you can love, stories you can remember. The stories were driven by plot and character, with grand heroes, terrible villains, beautiful damsels (often in distress), diabolical plots, amazing places, breathless romances. The readers wanted to be taken beyond the mundane, to live adventures far removed from their ordinary lives—and the pulps rarely failed to deliver.

In that regard, pulp fiction stands in the tradition of all memorable literature. For as history has shown, good stories are much more than fancy prose. William Shakespeare, Charles Dickens, Jules Verne, Alexandre Dumas—many of the greatest literary figures wrote their fiction for the readers, not simply literary colleagues and academic admirers. And writers for pulp magazines were no exception. These publications reached an audience that dwarfed the circulations of today's short story magazines. Issues of the pulps were scooped up and read by over thirty million avid readers each month.

Because pulp fiction writers were often paid no more than a cent a word, they had to become prolific or starve. They also had to write aggressively. As Richard Kyle, publisher and editor of *Argosy,* the first and most long-lived of the pulps, so pointedly explained: "The pulp magazine writers, the best of them, worked for markets that did not write for critics or attempt to satisfy timid advertisers. Not having to answer to anyone other than their readers, they wrote about human beings on the edges of the unknown, in those new lands the future would explore. They wrote for what we would become, not for what we had already been."

Some of the more lasting names that graced the pulps include H. P. Lovecraft, Edgar Rice Burroughs, Robert E. Howard, Max Brand, Louis L'Amour, Elmore Leonard, Dashiell Hammett, Raymond Chandler, Erle Stanley Gardner, John D. MacDonald, Ray Bradbury, Isaac Asimov, Robert Heinlein—and, of course, L. Ron Hubbard.

In a word, he was among the most prolific and popular writers of the era. He was also the most enduring—hence this series—and certainly among the most legendary. It all began only months after he first tried his hand at fiction, with L. Ron Hubbard tales appearing in *Thrilling Adventures, Argosy, Five-Novels Monthly, Detective Fiction Weekly, Top-Notch, Texas Ranger, War Birds, Western Stories,* even *Romantic Range.* He could write on any subject, in any genre, from jungle explorers to deep-sea divers, from G-men and gangsters, cowboys and flying aces to mountain climbers, hard-boiled detectives and spies. But he really began to shine when he turned his talent to science fiction and fantasy of which he authored nearly fifty novels or novelettes to forever change the shape of those genres.

Following in the tradition of such famed authors as Herman Melville, Mark Twain, Jack London and Ernest Hemingway, Ron Hubbard actually lived adventures that his own characters would have admired—as an ethnologist among primitive tribes, as prospector and engineer in hostile climes, as a captain of vessels on four oceans. He even wrote a series of articles for *Argosy,* called "Hell Job," in which he lived and told of the most dangerous professions a man could put his hand to.

Finally, and just for good measure, he was also an accomplished photographer, artist, filmmaker, musician and educator. But he was first and foremost a *writer,* and that's the L. Ron Hubbard we come to know through the pages of this volume.

This library of Stories from the Golden Age presents the best of L. Ron Hubbard's fiction from the heyday of storytelling, the Golden Age of the pulp magazines. In these eighty volumes, readers are treated to a full banquet of 153 stories, a kaleidoscope of tales representing every imaginable genre: science fiction, fantasy, western, mystery, thriller, horror, even romance—action of all kinds and in all places.

Because the pulps themselves were printed on such inexpensive paper with high acid content, issues were not meant to endure. As the years go by, the original issues of every pulp from *Argosy* through *Zeppelin Stories* continue crumbling into brittle, brown dust. This library preserves the L. Ron Hubbard tales from that era, presented with a distinctive look that brings back the nostalgic flavor of those times.

L. Ron Hubbard's Stories from the Golden Age has something for every taste, every reader. These tales will return you to a time when fiction was good clean entertainment and the most fun a kid could have on a rainy afternoon or the best thing an adult could enjoy after a long day at work.

Pick up a volume, and remember what reading is supposed to be all about. Remember curling up with a *great story.*

—Kevin J. Anderson

KEVIN J. ANDERSON *is the author of more than ninety critically acclaimed works of speculative fiction, including The Saga of Seven Suns, the continuation of the Dune Chronicles with Brian Herbert, and his* New York Times *bestselling novelization of L. Ron Hubbard's* Ai! Pedrito!

Tomb of the Ten Thousand Dead

CHAPTER ONE

The Pottery Jar

I have been asked to tell this story a hundred times. I have only told it once—to the British government, when they were quizzing me about the slaughter of the Lancaster-Mallard Expedition to Makran, Baluchistan.

My part was a major one only because I was the only man who escaped with his life. And that was strange because I had no real interest whatever in the findings of this expedition.

I am a pilot. Let it suffice to say that I was hired by Lancaster, a professor in a small Midwestern college, to pilot the cabin job they had bought across these awful wastes.

The expedition was boring most of the time until . . .

Tyler lay on his face in front of my tent. The morning sun was shining upon half the blade of a dagger. A spreading stain welled out over his back. Furrows were in the sand where his hands had clawed in the last agonies of death.

I blinked in the morning sunlight, unable to realize that young Tyler was really dead. No one had any reason to murder him. He was harmless, good humored. I was seized with the awful premonition that I might be next. Something was afoot, something horrible.

I stepped over the stones and knelt beside him, looking

at the knife. In the silence I could hear his watch ticking, *clickety-click*. Funny that it was still running while Tyler was dead. Funny that a machine should outlast its master.

Dazed by the sudden discovery, I looked blankly about me. A small pottery container was lying on the earth beside him. I remembered seeing it before. It had contained some document Mallard had unearthed.

I put out my hand to touch the knife.

"Don't touch it!" a voice behind me cried. "I've got you, Gordon. I've got you!"

Amazed, I turned slowly and stared into the muzzle of a revolver. Mallard's hand was shaking and his eyes were cold. He had me covered and I did not know why.

He was a big-headed, narrow-shouldered man. He was the kind you see poring over ancient skulls and ancient pottery finds in museums. He was as dry as the dust of the bones he found.

"Put away the gun," I said.

Lancaster, a brawny giant with a black beard, came out of his tent and stood there, staring at the tableau.

"Look what Gordon's done," said Mallard in a shaking voice.

"Wait a minute," I cried. "What do you mean by that? My God, Mallard, I know you've been ill and that you're upset, but don't get the idea that I'd kill Tyler."

Lancaster's eyes were baleful as he looked at the dead man. "I think you did. You quarreled with him the other day. No use to try to lie out of it, Gordon. We've got the drop on you. Here, what's this?"

Lancaster stooped and picked up the vase. He looked inside. "It's empty! Damn you, Gordon, where's that map?"

This was all coming too thick and fast for me. I stood up. "Don't jump at conclusions, Lancaster. I know nothing about your damned map."

"He's stalling," said Mallard. "He knows what that map means. He knows we've come out here to find—"

"Shut up," barked Lancaster. "Gordon, you'll throw your revolver this way and you'll march into your tent and stay there, understand? We're holding you for Tyler's murder."

Our native guide, a Dehwar named Kehlar, shuffled out of the cook tent and leaned indolently against a pole. He had an amused expression on his face.

"You won't shoot, Mallard," I said. "In the first place you haven't got the nerve, and in the next place, if anything happened to me, who'd fly that plane out of here? I'm the only man here who can fly and if I'm killed, you'll starve in this desert. This place has swallowed up the better part of three armies. There isn't a water hole for fifty miles. Go on and shoot, Mallard."

I walked toward him, deliberately. I thought I had the upper hand for the moment. Suddenly Lancaster dived for me.

He was bigger than I was and when he hit me I skidded ten feet through the coarse sand. I lit with him on top of me. He started to let me have it with his fist, but I jackknifed and threw him away from me.

Mallard stood back, gun limp in his hand, an expectant stare masking his nervousness.

Lancaster flipped and came at me again. Sand spurted in tan geysers when he hit the ground beside me. He whipped one into my jaw and sent me reeling.

The ferocity of his attack was something which would not be withstood. His hands were great things, as big as basketballs, and when those knuckles struck they left a deep and heavy mark.

I tried to make my wiriness count as much as I could, but it was a losing fight from the first. I had to stand up and slug with him.

His fists came like cannonballs and each time he landed on my body or face, great, round lights soared up and exploded behind my eyes. He was standing there, letting me have it, and I couldn't get away. I tensed myself for one good crack at the point of his jaw before he knocked me out.

I let drive and connected so hard that it numbed my whole arm. He rocked on his heels and then crouched down. I struck again, furiously. Blood pinked his cheek.

He cuffed out with his hairy fist and rocked me into a pile of stones. I staggered up, stunned, and walked into his left. He sent me reeling again. I could taste hot, salty blood.

I went down into the swirling dust and Lancaster kicked me deliberately in the side. Mallard brought out a length of rope. They held me down and tied my hands behind me. Kehlar, unmoved, helped them carry me into the tent.

I spat out a mouthful of blood. "You'll have a hell of a time getting out of here without me," I raged.

"I think you'll fly us out," said Lancaster with a growl.

"You'll fly us far enough when we want you to. And we'll turn you over to the British and let them hang you for this. I think that's best. Yes, and it's simple. You'll fly and when we contact a British patrol, we'll turn you over to them for trial and execution."

"You are correct," said Mallard in his weak, piping voice. "I came out and saw him kneeling there, making sure that Tyler was dead."

"He's been too sly, anyway," said Lancaster. "Maybe if we search his stuff we'll find the map."

They searched and failed to find anything but shaving cream and a pair of socks I had thought long lost. They finally gave up and posted Kehlar outside the tent with a rifle to make sure I didn't get away.

And there I was, in the center of the Makran wastes, on my back and helpless, waiting for a British patrol.

And who would believe an unknown pilot when his word was stacked against that of two eminent scientists?

Nobody.

That was the way it all started. And I lay there while the sun fanned down its barrage of heat and cursed the flies, Lancaster, Mallard and Kehlar.

We had been scouting this bleak section for months, looking into the archaeology and ethnology of the place. So far we had had little trouble. Mallard and Lancaster, spouting Latin and Persian and Greek, had dug happily in the sands and scorching rocks, getting excited over bits of pottery and other relics of the past. Tyler had not had much enthusiasm for that sort of thing. He had been more interested in the material, adventurous side of life.

Tyler had been in bad several times. He was the black sheep of the expedition. I minded my own business because I was too tired from nerve strain to do anything else. Tyler had had additional energy. Several times he had been in fights with the natives over women and such, but I had liked his devil-may-care way of doing things. He always had a grin which contrasted wonderfully with the sour expressions of the two professors.

And now Tyler was probably wooing the angels and getting the dickens for it, and I was lying here in the heat, swearing and going mad with the flies.

After a little I quieted down and began to wonder who would pilot the cabin plane if I wasn't there. Neither Mallard nor Lancaster knew anything about flying, as evidenced by their demands that I land in impossible places so that they could inspect their beloved mounds.

Moral people, Lancaster and Mallard. They had always lectured Tyler on his taste for living and had always reproved me for my lack of interest in ancient things. They thought we should have availed ourselves of this beautiful chance to improve our minds and we had not.

Then I began to think that this was a rather flimsy excuse for nailing me down this way. They knew that I liked Tyler. Why had they suddenly turned on me like that?

Certainly these men were not so foolish as to think they could get away with anything under British law. Certainly they realized that without that plane they would be in a bad spot.

You don't just start out and walk through Makran. Tens of centuries ago some people tried it. The mythical woman scourge named Semiramis had started into it with an army and had come out of it with nothing but her life. Cyrus the Great had entered it unadvisedly and had lost his army to a man.

Water was so scarce as to almost be nonexistent. The dry, wasted, rolling dunes and gray rock were without habitations. Only at dawn was it cool and then so briefly that it only succeeded in accentuating the daily scorch.

Frankly, at the time I knew nothing about this map they had found. Who cared about a map when you had to keep an engine ticking under these terrific conditions? When you had to shoot landings along runways so studded with rock that the smoothest glide turned into a pogo-stick race as you touched?

But they had found this thing and now Tyler was dead and the only thing I knew was that such a map must be damned valuable.

I heard shovels clicking and knew that they were burying Tyler, giving him an unmarked grave under these foreign skies, so far from his native Virginia. It angered me and I did not reason that you don't leave the dead out in the sun. Not in the deserts of the Makran.

Soon Lancaster and Mallard departed to inspect a mound we had sighted the night before. I had noticed something feverish about them when we spotted it. But then they got that way on the slightest provocation. They would jabber for hours over a piece of junk I could have bought for a dime near any Hopi village at home.

Maybe education makes men that way. A mere pilot couldn't be expected to understand.

CHAPTER TWO

The Knife Fighter

I could see Kehlar's shadow on the canvas wall. He was leaning on the rifle, waiting until the white men were out of sight before he took a nap.

I knew Kehlar. He was a strong brute, light fingered and greasy, a crossbreed of Tajik and Arab and Dehwar. His eyes were shifty but he had a bold front. He wore dirty robes and a Punjab turban.

I knew I had to get loose from there. I began to work at my wrist ropes. It was a good thing to have small hands. By pulling up the slight slack in the rope, I managed to slip my cuffs.

I was about to get up when I saw Kehlar's shadow begin to move. He came stealthily, carrying the gun as though he wanted to use it. I lay back and pretended to sleep.

He lifted the flap of the tent and shoved his dirty face into the slit. He stood there and assured himself that I was not dangerous. He hefted the rifle and came forward.

When he leaned over me I let him have it. I doubled up like a jackknife and rammed my heels into his stomach. With a mighty kick I sent him sprawling across the tent, shaking the frail structure as though a cyclone had hit it. Leaping up I tried to dive at him and put him out of action, but my foot caught in a blanket and threw me flat on the floor.

Kehlar acted on impulse. He brought up the rifle butt and drove its hell down at my face, hard and fast, to drive my nose through the back of my head. But at the last instant I managed to roll aside and the butt kicked up dirt beside my ear.

Snatching at Kehlar's boots, I pulled him down on top of me. He struggled and dropped the rifle. His hand was at his belt and he fought to get out his knife.

I was almost smothered in his robes. He smelled like long-dead sheep.

He had his knife. I saw it flash over me. He drove it down at my side. With a frenzied effort I managed to capture his wrist and hold it back.

His teeth were bared in a snarl. He was berserk and his strength was terrific. Nothing could hold that wrist for long.

With my free hand I slammed a body blow at him. He went limp for a second and I gave him another one. The knife went spinning and I threw him aside.

Kehlar knew he was losing the fight now. He was plainly scared. He leaped back, trying to get out of the tent.

He struck a pole and the ridge bowed dangerously. Abruptly the whole thing came down, wrapping us up in its heavy folds.

I felt something scratching around behind me. Kehlar was trying to find his knife. I dived for him but only managed to get an armload of canvas.

The sharp blade was in his hand now. It pierced the canvas an inch from my face. This was no place for me, and while he freed his knife, I clawed out of the confining tent and drew a deep breath of air.

I hadn't finished him yet. He knew I was outside and with the knife to lend him courage, he was coming after me.

In an instant he burst out before me, knife raised. I drove a fist under the blade and sidestepped at the same time. It was a clean, lucky blow. I let him have another one as he went down.

I had only one thought in mind, I had to get out of there and get to a British outpost and bring order out of this chaos.

Hastily I crammed some food into a bag, picked up the water canteens and ran toward the plane. I threw the water bags into the cabin and threw on the mags. I went around and pulled the prop through. It was hot enough, that motor. The sun was enough to burn you into charcoal.

Nothing came of the pull and I tried again.

"Sand," I said to myself.

I expected Mallard and Lancaster to come back any minute. I had to work like the devil if I wanted to get out of here without having a murder pinned on me. If I got to the British first I had a chance to make my story stick.

Nothing happened the second and third time. Fuming, I glanced at the intake lines. A section was missing!

Damn them! They knew I might get out. They hadn't trusted Kehlar. I had to get that brass line before I could escape.

In a frenzy I cut around the wing and came back to the pit. Maybe I had some spare brass tubing. Anything to make that engine percolate.

I had forgotten Kehlar.

In the toolbox I discovered the makings of a water condenser. I whipped off the tubing and began to fix the connections.

Somehow I had to get it to work. My life and reputation were at stake.

For fifteen minutes I worked there, sweating and swearing and then I had it almost finished. In another few seconds I would be starting the engine and getting out.

A soft voice behind me, a voice filled with careless menace, said, "Do not move, please."

I whirled to face Kehlar. He had the rifle and stood there covering me with it. His face was bloody and he looked as though the merest spark would contract the trigger.

"I have a kind heart," said Kehlar. "I need you and I will not shoot if you give me your word not to start fighting again."

"You need me?"

"Yes, and I will make you rich beyond all dreams. Quick, Gordon. They may come back."

"All right. I give you my word," I said wearily.

Kehlar laughed at me and threw open the magazine. The rifle was empty. He thought it was a good joke and I had half a mind to throttle him.

In an instant he grew serious again. "Listen, Gordon, I have that thing which they need. They did not think I would take it. I let them search me and I had buried it in the sand meanwhile. Here it is."

He knelt quickly and spread out a piece of material, perhaps papyrus, on which several lines were traced, designated by Greek words.

"I will be quick with you," said Kehlar. "I think I can trust you. These men are after the treasure left here by Iskander of the Two Horns, the man you know as Alexander the Great who crossed this desert twenty-three centuries ago when he came back from India. Do you understand?"

Did I understand? I was way ahead of him.

"This," said Kehlar, "is the map we found in that jar near Pasni. Alexander left it there with his soldiers. This shows how he marched from Ras Malan to this place we stopped northwest of here, called Pasni.

"See? There is the coast and here is his line of march. He was coming back from India and he wanted to travel along this coast on account of the fleet he had, but he had to go inland at Ras Malan and cross this desert.

"He was very foolish to do that. This desert is no place for any army as you understand, eh? But he had fifty, sixty thousand men, lots of camp followers. They get sick and die. He got a lot of Greek soldiers and they die. He got a lot of women and they die. They starve and eat the mules and horses and maybe elephants. And"—Kehlar paused and licked his lips—"he could not carry all the millions he had looted in India on the backs of his men and—"

"He left it here!" I cried.

"That is right," said Kehlar. "He left it here. He built a sort of house for all this loot out of India and he left it here. This map shows that—"

Ka-pow!

The crack of the rifle was hollow in the emptiness of the desert. My helmet went spinning.

A second shot plopped down between us. Kehlar leaped

15

to his feet and grabbed the water bags. I ran after him and dived into the shelter of a sand dune. We floundered along in the cover, making for another dune.

"Them fellows mean plenty business," panted Kehlar.

"Who?"

"I don't know. Maybe white men, huh? Maybe they think we going to kill them. Well, maybe we will."

For about an hour we made our torturous way through these temporary canyons which sifted with the wind. A young gale was blowing up, kicking at the sand and tearing yellow plumes off the crests. The drift was covering our tracks.

It was quite evident in that walk that neither of us trusted the other. Neither of us dared fall behind so much as a foot. Clutched in Kehlar's hand was plenty of motive for death.

The loot of India!

Millions!

It never occurred to me that if Alexander couldn't get it out, a less brilliant mortal might also suffer defeat in spite of modern equipment. No, I let all that rest as it was. I was interested only in getting to that mound and finding a way inside.

Oh, for a steam shovel and a crew of strong backs.

Against the sky ahead, the low mound crouched like some great beast waiting to devour anyone who came within reach of its scorching walls. Somewhere behind us, Lancaster and Mallard—or maybe somebody else—were determined upon our destruction.

I was dizzy with sun and dopey with thoughts of vast sums. But I watched Kehlar. Things began to shape up. Poor Tyler.

He'd suffered months of boredom and now when something exciting came he was dead.

It wasn't the first time I had dreamed wild dreams about becoming immensely wealthy. When they needed pilots to get machinery and men into Great Bear Lake, I was behind a throttle and stick, hoping to make a strike of my own. And when I did not, then I was in Colombia, freighting stuff over the Andes. There in Colombia I had vague ideas about emeralds, but I never saw any.

And now here I was, again on the trail of easy wealth. It takes a man a long time to learn that there is no such animal.

We skirted the base of the mound and found it taller than we had suspected at first. The heaping sands had covered it over with great thoroughness as though anxious to safeguard a trust given twenty-three centuries before.

The wind was picking up in velocity and the sand was stinging and bitter against our cheeks. It got between our teeth and into our eyes. I had the edge on Kehlar. I had a pair of goggles, he had only his Punjab turban.

"Now," said Kehlar above the singing whine of the wind and shifting sand, "now we are here, how do we get in?"

I scrambled up the far side of the mound, ankles deep in sand, and stared toward the camp. I could see nothing in that direction. The flying sand was too thick. A good thing, I thought, I had been so careful in tying down the cabin job. We were going to need it in a hurry very shortly.

But seeing nothing did not mean that we were safe. Mallard and Lancaster were out there in the dunes somewhere scouting for us with rifles. I was certain of that. They were not inclined to allow anyone to disturb one of the greatest archaeological finds which would ever be made, one of the greatest of all time.

When I came down shaking my head, Kehlar looked about and with nervous haste, began to claw at the sand. But every time he scooped out a hole, the wind filled it instantly. The sand was too dry to be dug. I realized with a sinking stomach that it might take weeks and weeks to clear this mound entirely. Certainly no building would last twenty-three centuries.

We would find only the ruins beneath.

CHAPTER THREE

The Gems of Alexander

W E crouched down out of the wind and Kehlar again consulted his map. He pursed his thick lips and pulled at his beard, eyes half closed as he studied. Finally he glanced up at the sun which hung over us like a cauldron upended and got his direction.

"The north side," said Kehlar. "Entrance on the north side."

"But we'll need shovels," I protested. "We can't make any headway in this wind."

"We got to make headway," said Kehlar. "Them white men don't like us to fool with this place. I know. They crazy. Gold make everybody crazy."

I had an idea then. There were many large rocks lying about and with them it would be no great trick to build a low wall up the side of the mound. I explained my plan to Kehlar and, somewhat mystified, he helped me.

Before we had laid a dozen boulders, I could see success ahead. By laying this wall before the wind, the action of the diverted air could be made to work like a compressed air hose. Great hollows began to appear behind the wall, scooped out by the whining wind.

Soon we began to see some kind of order in the uncovered rocks and knew that we were getting to the inner wall.

We moved the barricade a little and the uncovering process

went on. And then, finally, we saw a small hole in the side of the mound. Working eagerly with our hands we scooped out the sand, enlarged the place, and I wriggled in through the opening.

It was pitch black inside. Kehlar came through into the silence of the place and stood beside me, breathing hard. I fended unconsciously with my hand in case he saw fit to do things with a knife, but he was evidently too engrossed in the surroundings.

Kehlar pulled out a pocket torch he had stolen from the plane and clicked on the switch. The pale beam stabbed through the blackness and glanced off a wall.

I was rooted to the spot by what I saw. Alexander the Great had been in a hurry when he crossed this desert and yet he had paused long enough to build or cause to be built the model of a Greek temple out of crude stones. No pillars, of course, but the square room's design was unmistakable.

It was a shock to find this thing here. All the mounds I had seen uncovered had disclosed broken masonry and perhaps a few flagstones which had once been a floor. But this was built so ruggedly that, with its protecting cloak of sand, it had withstood twenty-three centuries of erosion.

And then my spirits fell. "Look, Kehlar, somebody has beat us to it. It's empty!"

Kehlar began to swear in lurid Baluchi. The beam of light threshed about like a tiger's tail but we could see nothing of the reputed loot of India. Instead of bags of riches, we had an empty vault. No matter the archaeological value. You can't spend history.

"That's that," I said in a weary voice. "Let Mallard and Lancaster have it, all of it. To think that Tyler was killed over a farce like this!"

"No, no!" cried Kehlar in protest. "It must be here. It has to be here. For years without number my people have searched for this place. We would know if it had been stripped."

I began to feel uneasy in the tomblike darkness. Something like a chill passed over me and made the running rivulets of sweat which coursed under my khaki turn to glacial streams. My voice was shaky when I said, "Let's get out of here, Kehlar."

But he would not be so easily defeated. Kehlar envisioned himself as a sultan, surrounded by jewels and women, wanting for nothing. Kehlar's small eyes were greedy and his mouth twitched with the effort of thought.

"We look farther," he said. In the velvet gloom his voice had a meticulous quality. He was being wary. He, too, felt the vague presence of disaster.

You know how you feel when you are certain something horrible is about to happen to you. Your belly gets tight and you shake and look over your shoulder and try to fasten upon the danger without quite being able to do so.

That's the way I felt. Death was in the shrieking wind outside. Death crouched in these dark corners.

I stalked across the floor, trying to shake off the fear by making unimportant noises. My boot heels rang hollowly on the flags. Kehlar stood tense, listening. Perhaps he heard something outside. The beam of light remained motionless, giving a blue cast to his face.

"The floor," he whispered hoarsely. "The floor's hollow!"

21

I rapped again with my heels. I seemed to feel the stone give a little. Excitedly I crouched down and tore at the blocks with my fingers, stripping off the nails without noticing that blood flowed.

The loot of India! Alexander had died before he needed to send for it. Here it was, underfoot. My hopes were high when the stone began to give. Kehlar was down there beside me, tugging and hauling at the stone.

Suddenly I felt the floor tip. A block had loosed itself from the others.

Backwards, clawing for a hold, I fell through blackness. I did not know what was beneath me. I had no way of seeing where I would eventually land.

Something was falling with me. A beam of light was twisting itself upwards. Even as I plummeted down I knew that I had torn the flashlight from Kehlar's grasp.

I hit on my back and shoulders and rolled to lessen the fall. The wind was gone out of me and for some seconds I lay wheezing in the dark. I remembered hearing a tinkle as I landed. Feeling about, I discovered the flashlight was broken beyond repair.

"Kehlar!"

He answered me instantly. "Turn on the flashlight and help me down!"

"There isn't any flashlight. It's broken. Give me your hands!"

I heard a scratching sound over me but try as I might I could not contact him. It was twelve feet to the next level.

"I go for a rope and more light," said Kehlar.

Panic hit me then. If anything happened to Kehlar I would be forever entombed.

"Wait," I begged. "I'll try to jump it."

Four times I hurtled through blackness and four times I missed, succeeding only in scraping off a large area of skin.

"You wait," said Kehlar. "I come back."

He left me then and I could hear him moving above. The horror of being left alone here in the blackness, perhaps to starve, struck me.

Without thinking that I might never get back to the trap overhead and without realizing that Alexander might have been more thorough in his building than I imagined, I felt along the walls, trying to find something to stand upon.

The air was dry and the floor was covered with thick sand which had somehow drifted in. I knelt once and felt something sting my knee. Jumping up in alarm I examined that scraped member and found nothing wrong with it. There must be salt in this sand. But then, of course, this dry waste might have once been part of the Arabian Sea.

Wandering on I tripped over an object hidden by the dark. Kneeling again I ran my fingers over the thing. But then I was not used to being blind. My fingers only told me that the object was rough, angular and hard.

On I went, sometimes falling, completely lost as to direction. I was under the impression that I was traveling around a circular vault. I kept telling myself that Kehlar would soon come back.

How was I to know that Kehlar . . .

Again I tripped and something clanked beside me. I felt it and as near as I could make out it was a helmet of some ancient pattern. My questing fingers encountered another thing.

Hair! Human hair!

I knew, then. I knew that I was in a vault with dead men all about me and under me, on every side of me. Hundreds, perhaps thousands of dead men.

In the moment which followed, reaction had not hit me. On my knees I began to dig in the soft, dry sand. I touched something which felt like a face. I touched a foot, another helmet, a sword . . .

Then it was true! I was walking on bodies twenty-three centuries dead.

Hysteria didn't hit me. Not yet. My thoughts flowed on connectedly. Alexander could do these things. He could cause a vault to be built here in this forgotten waste to house his Macedonian veterans who had succumbed in his long campaign eastward. He had given them decent burial and . . . Had he stored his loot here?

My hand contacted cold teeth then and I leaped up, back to the wall. I could see nothing and I could hear the blood pounding in my head, roaring like a mad river. Sweat poured from me.

Twenty-three centuries dead! That was the feeling I had had. Some sixth sense had told me that when we had entered the tomb. The grisly mummies were under me, around me. I could feel the hard spots in the sand now and I knew what they were. Dry sand and salt had done a better job than any Egyptian doctor.

Behind me I heard a soft, sinuous sound.

Were there snakes in this place? Could it be that . . . No, men twenty-three centuries dead do not move and walk. Or did they?

The sound came again. It was a footstep, repeated time after time. Something was moving through this darkness toward me, creeping up on me as though it could see me while I remained blind and stifled.

Then the darkness began to glow and I realized that this was a narrow place in the vault and that whatever was coming came from around a corner. It was moving slowly, slowly, as though anxious not to frighten me away before it could kill me.

Was this the price of violating the tomb of Alexander's Macedonians? Was this some dried horror creeping up on me?

I moved and a helmet rattled under my feet. The light went out suddenly and the footsteps ceased.

I ran my fingers through the sand and found the helmet. It was coldly solid in my grasp. Without knowing why I did so I replaced my lost headgear with it. Perhaps I had some idea of protecting my skull. Again I searched in the dry grit, touching the icy flesh of the long-dead legionnaires.

A short weapon came into my grasp. I hefted it. The blade was dull but it had weight. I stood up then and listened intently. No longer could I hear the footsteps. A man could walk silently in that soft sand if he did not step on the equipment.

A hairy hand brushed my cheek. Quicker than a striking black panther the thing gripped me and hurled me down.

Too late I struck out with the sword. A guttural growl echoed through the vault as the thing swept down upon me.

Light was coming from somewhere. A faint glow which silhouetted this beastly thing over me. I rolled aside and felt something strike a glancing blow where I had been.

I reared up only to be battered back again. Stunned, I rolled once more, trying to get a grip on the treacherous sand. My heels fastened into something, perhaps a dead man. I struck with the short sword and felt it bite deep. Again and again I drove the blows into flesh and then, exhausted and gagging, reeled backward to support myself against the wall.

The thing had slumped down into the sand.

When I could breathe, I made my way toward the light. Turning an angle in the corridor I was instantly blinded by the glare before me. The man who held the flash let out a sharp gasp of terror.

The light swished away from me and in an instant I made out the figure of Kehlar. He was trying to get away, slipping over the sand and tripping.

"Kehlar! Wait!"

He stopped and turned around and the light played over me again. Then, as though still distrusting his eyes, he came hesitantly forward.

"Gordon," he whispered.

For an instant I was angry and then I realized that I wore the helmet and carried the sword of a Macedonian hoplite. My blood-smeared face beneath the greenish bronze helmet must have looked horrible, judging from Kehlar's expression.

When Kehlar gasped with relief I felt the tension of the place lessen around me. I grinned. Kehlar was soon over his shock and his attention immediately went to the sword.

I followed his glance and saw that this was not an ordinary weapon. It was, in short, an *acinaces* of the type carried by Persian nobles. Not much of the hilt was left, but the blade was there, untarnished. It was heavy because it was solid gold.

Greed flickered again in Kehlar's small eyes. He quickly went down the passage, taking care that I did not get too far behind him. He did not trust me any more than I trusted him.

My first thought was to examine with the aid of the flashlight the body of the thing I had killed. I wanted to assure myself that it was real. The soundless tomb was getting me again. Now I could see the mummified dead, preserved through twenty-three centuries by dry sand and salt. The sightless black faces were grisly. The skin was dried until it stretched across the cheekbones as tight as a drumhead.

Macedonian veterans, heroes of a thousand battles across the world, placed here by the hand of Alexander of the Two Horns, earthshaker.

I saw the tracks in the loose sand I had so lately made. They stopped in a swirl which marked the spot of the fight. I gasped and stepped back.

There was nothing there.

No blood.

Only the upturned face of a mummy.

Instantly the gruesome surroundings took hold of me. I did not want to go on. I wanted to go back to the light of day, away from these legions of dead men.

I did not tell Kehlar because I could not find my voice and because Kehlar was hauling at small, decayed chests from which spilled red and yellow flashes—waterfalls of precious stones.

Kehlar's greed recognized no fear now. He did not care for the dead. He hurled them impatiently aside like logs and kicked away the piles of green bronze armor.

Whipping off his burnoose, Kehlar began to pour the jewels upon it.

"Help me," he commanded. "Quick, we have not much time."

I tried to gather up some of the jewels, but I kept looking over my shoulders and staring at the mummies, expecting them to rise up to battle as they had so efficiently twenty-three centuries before.

Kehlar tied the ends of the cloak together and thrust the bundle at me.

"Take this back to the upper chamber and place it there. I get more."

Nerveless, I took the load—and it was heavier than I ever thought jewels could be. Fumbling along the wall, I made my way through the quiet vault, leaving Kehlar's light far behind me.

At length I discovered his ladder and, holding the bag in one hand, made my way up the rope strands. I laid the bundle on the floor above and crawled over the edge.

*"Take this back to the upper chamber and
place it there. I get more."*

CHAPTER FOUR

Tomb of the Macedonians

THE storm was still blowing outside. The noise was a relief after the silence below. Partly because I wanted to get outside, and partly because I did not wish to place such a valuable burden within, I wormed through the small hole and buried the bundle under the rock wall we had made, carefully marking the place with three stones forming a triangle above it.

Then I went back into the tomb, still carrying the sword in my belt.

Nothing happened when I slid down the rope ladder. Nothing happened when I worked my way along the dismal corridor which was carpeted with dead men who tripped me from time to time. Nothing happened when I spotted the glow of Kehlar's flashlight.

I realized then that the light was standing still, facing away from me, evidently lying on the floor. Dull apprehension gripped me as I slid forward.

I found Kehlar. He was lying on his face with outstretched hands. He was lying very still while blood seeped out of his left armpit and stained the sand.

A dagger protruded from the wound, driven down with terrific force. His heart was still, stopped by the bronze dagger.

I picked up the fallen light and looked at the motionless

faces of the dead about me. Somehow those faces seemed to be smiling, laughing at me.

Suddenly I was running, falling over clattering armor and wooden flesh. I was running and falling and running again. After a minute or two I reached the place where the ladder had been. It was gone!

Breathing hard, I stared up, trying to realize what had happened to me. I could not believe that I was trapped here with dead men who rose up and murdered with their ancient weapons. I could not believe that I had no way to get out.

Somehow I had to reach that opening many feet over my head. Somehow I had to get something high enough to put me there. I had no compunctions about the dead now. I had plenty of corpses.

I burrowed in the sand and began to stack the grisly things under the hole. I dragged them forth like so much driftwood and built steps of them. I was utterly mad with terror, but somehow I retained enough reason to complete the task.

Then, mounting up over those shriveled bodies which had once been the terror of Asia, I managed to reach the opening and haul myself out.

I stood up, intending to make for the door, but at the first stride I fell over something soft and yielding. Playing the light down I discovered Lancaster.

He was lying on his face like the others. The knife had been driven into the left side of his back with workmanlike precision. A surgeon could not have done a more accurate job of reaching the heart.

But this knife was different. It was made of good western steel.

Lancaster's face was ugly in death. I turned the light away.

Then I saw something which Kehlar and I had missed. We had gone down through a hole of our own making. But in the far side of the room I could see another hole, a square one in the wall, made by removing an upright slab.

From this a passage slanted down, the real entrance to the tombs. Something clicked in my mind then and I dived for the main entrance, anxious only to get out and get away. But before I could reach it, it turned dark and I saw that a man was coming through.

The room was half alight from the rays of the sun. I could see the man clearly now. I stood my ground, sword in hand, and waited for him.

He stood up and started forward and then his eyes grew accustomed to the light and he saw me.

For seconds neither of us moved. His eyes grew wider and wider and his jaw began to slack. His mouth gaped blackly and I could see him shake with mounting terror.

I knew then what he thought. Mallard was not staring at Gordon, a pilot. He thought he was looking at one of Alexander's Macedonian veterans come back from twenty-three centuries beyond the veil. His sun-dazzled eyes could not see more than the greenish helmet I wore, the sword and the blood-smeared face.

He let out a crazy yell and dropped to his knees. He screamed and clutched at his gun.

I had not seen the gun before. I saw it now. It spat long streams of sparks and between the shots, Mallard's voice racked the tomb with repeated cries of tortured horror.

The first shot took me above the left elbow. I tried to lunge forward to get at him before he killed me. His next shot ripped through my thigh.

I knew that I had to kill him before he killed me.

I staggered across the floor, clutching the short sword, trying to keep the world from careening about me. He saw me come at him through the swirling cloud of powder smoke. His mouth was drooling and his eyes were wild with fear.

With my last ounce of willpower I dived at him and hacked down with that dull blade. His skull cracked like an eggshell, spilling out his thick blood. He folded up like an empty sack and lay flat against the floor, arms contracting and relaxing as he died.

I stumbled to my knees in front of him, still expecting him to rise up and shoot again. But he was motionless. Mallard was finished.

I was conscious of the wet, sticky blood which welled out of me. With careful deliberation I sat up and began to rip Mallard's shirt into tourniquets. I had some difficulty in getting them on. I was numb with shock and the pain wasn't bad. Not yet.

With a strange calm I searched Mallard for the fuel line and found it. His face, I noticed, was badly bruised and several welts appeared on his bared shoulders.

My mind seemed to work with a strange clarity as I sat

there. I was thinking better than I ever had before. It was like a light bulb which flares up just before it goes out.

I had given him that welt on his face and those shoulder bruises down in the tomb. Mallard was the strange thing which had attacked me. I had merely stunned him and he had had time to get away.

Mallard was behind all that. Mallard was the killer.

Funny how clear it was to me now as I sat there on my heels, sopping at the blood which poured out of me. I knew the whole story in the blink of an eye.

I was not worried as to how I would get out of there. Not yet. I was pleased with myself over making this discovery.

Tyler had been killed by Mallard an instant before I had come out of the tent. Kehlar had stolen the map from Mallard during the night, had broken the jar and thrown it away just outside my tent as he escaped.

Tyler had come along and picked up the pottery jar and Mallard had seen him. Mallard, unbalanced by the loss of the map and by the thought of Alexander's millions, having schemed and planned already to get everything for himself, had thought to recover the map from Tyler by knifing the boy.

Suddenly realizing that the jar was empty, and hearing me approach, Mallard had dived into his tent, had come out and charged me with the murder.

He had remembered too late that he needed me to fly the crate for him. But he had determined that I should not get away at any cost. He needed me and if I was tied up he would have me. He would make me land somewhere at the point of a gun and would have finished me on the spot, destroying me and the plane together and then stumbling into some outpost with a pack of lies.

When Mallard had come back from the tomb to find that I had escaped, he was panic-stricken and he shot at me, hoping to come close and still miss, hoping to make me surrender to him.

Lancaster was scouting on his own. Mallard had no further use for Lancaster. He had gone off looking for the other professor and failed to find him.

Instead, Mallard had found that other entrance into the underground passages. He had come down, had seen me and had thought me to be Lancaster. He had tried to murder me but I had stunned him with the sword.

Then Mallard had wandered around underground and had at last come back to find Kehlar sorting out the jewels and had promptly knifed him from the back. Going above ground by the other route and missing me, Mallard had located Lancaster about to descend by my rope ladder. He had killed Lancaster because he saw now that he had to wipe out all evidence against himself. He was mad with greed.

But he was worried about me. Without a pilot he would be left to die in this desert and he had gone outside to make sure of me. When he had returned to find a Macedonian soldier confronting him, he was too unnerved to do anything but shoot.

Yes, I had it all now. Mallard had known he would do this from the first, had planned it all out so that he alone would have this wealth. He was insane with desire for money and power. He had had nothing all his life. Well, never mind. He was dead.

My strength was going fast. I had to get out of there, but the instant I moved, pain swamped me. But I had to get help and treatment for these wounds.

I tried to go back into the tomb for the treasure, but everything grew black before my eyes. The light bulb had gone out.

I tried to think and could not. I have a vague memory of straining to install the fuel line, succeeding somehow.

Writhing in agony I somehow got off the ground. I remember that much dimly. Then all I can recall is a red sheet of misery dropped before my eyes.

They tell me a fishing boat picked me up off the point of Ras el Kuh. They tell me there was no sign of a plane there. They tell me I was taken to an outpost up the gulf and removed to the Teheran hospital by military plane.

I don't know.

Weeks afterward I found myself in Teheran with two broken legs and a badly smashed arm and a gash which had almost taken off my scalp. When I recovered I borrowed a ship off the British and went back to look at the Makran in an attempt to discover the tomb again. But I had not counted on the things sandstorms do.

Evidently the whole camp had been blown down and covered up. The tomb was no different than a thousand other mounds in the vicinity. I could not find it at all.

They say it is useless to try. The map is down there in the velvet dark with Kehlar. Down there with those mummified bodies of the Macedonian legionnaires.

Someday someone may find the place again by chance. Perhaps it will not be opened for another twenty-three centuries.

Whoever opens it will be puzzled by the presence of Kehlar's corpse, no matter how many centuries intervene. Lancaster and Mallard will not last. They are not surrounded by salt and dry sand the way Kehlar and the legionnaires are. Yes, salt and dry sand make the best mummies. All the Egyptian kings knew that. A corpse so packed will last through eternity, faultlessly preserved.

Mummies? Yes, I came within an ace of staying there in that tomb, growing hard and stiff and dry, waiting for some adventurer to open up the place, even as I opened it.

Price of a Hat

Price of a Hat

WE were throwing cards into Stuart's wastebasket. Each of us had half a deck with different backs and the loser was paying all. It was a simple game, but anything was better than sitting around the studio listening to the sizzle and hiss of rain.

Stuart collected the cards, turning the wastebasket upside down. It was a queer contraption, that basket. It was small at the top and big at the bottom and it was covered with fur. And then I saw that it wasn't a wastebasket at all, but a *kubanka*.

"That's a funny-looking hat," I remarked.

The others eyed the object and Stuart turned it around in his hands, gazing thoughtfully at it.

"But not a very funny hat," said Stuart, slowly. "I don't know why I keep it around. Every time I pick it up I get a case of the jitters. But it cost too much to throw away."

That was odd, I thought. Stuart was a big chap with a very square face and a pocket full of money. He bought anything he happened to want and money meant nothing to him. But here he was talking about cost.

"Where'd you get it?" I demanded.

Still holding the thing, still looking at it, Stuart sat down in a big chair. "I've had it for a long, long time, but I don't know why. It spilled more blood than a dozen such hats could hold, and you see that this could hold a lot."

Something mournful in his tone made us take seats about him. Stuart usually joked about such things.

Back in 1917 (said Stuart) I was ordered out as a military observer—or perhaps as a spy—to Siberia. I spoke some Russian and they thought I could play the part and they had to have information.

You see, Russia was breaking up into chunks. For over a year things had been going badly, what with several governments and several revolutions, and the Allies were very much afraid that the Germans were mobilizing somewhere in the Urals.

You remember we had a couple Philippine regiments there and the British had about two thousand and the Japanese had put upwards of seventy thousand in the field against the Reds. It was all one grand diplomatic hodgepodge.

The idea was to get Russia back into shape so that the Russian troops would hold the German troops away from the Western Front.

Some forty-five thousand Czech soldiers, deserters from the Austrian forces, had been sent east across Siberia at their own request, but somehow the Reds and some German prisoners who were going west tangled up with a trainload of the Czechs and the Czechs, without country perhaps, but with good rifles just the same, decided that Russia should be straightened out.

So we had Japs and Yanks and Tommies and Czechs all fighting the Reds. And we had the Whites on our side. Siberia, for the most part, was in Czech hands and we had high hopes of setting Russia's house in order.

In the early part of July, 1918, I was sent into the eastern Urals, toward what was then Ekaterinburg, but which has been renamed Sverdlovsk. No one knew who was in charge of the town or who had it and I was supposed to find out.

I did and came back riding hell-for-leather, nursing a clipped arm. I hadn't even been in the town, but the Reds were looking for a fight all about it.

The Allies were getting worried about the *tsar*. He had been arrested months before and had not been heard from since. And although we hardly approved of Nicholas II as a ruler, we needed a head for the state we thought we could form and the best marionette we could find would be Nicholas—or maybe the *tsarevich*.

It was a very beautiful country and a beautiful day. The breeze was moaning through the firs and the sun was clear in a blue sky. Because I was all out of sorts at having to report bad news concerning Ekaterinburg, I stopped and watered my horse and sat down on a knoll, looking through the sloping forests and thinking sourly on all this hideous mess.

I remember it was the seventeenth of July—but then I thought the date meant nothing. As a matter of fact, the only meaning the date had was that it was followed by the eighteenth, if you understand me.

I had not been there long when I heard a series of shots

down one of the passes. Presently I heard a horse crashing through the woods and I caught the flash of a red cape. Another shot rapped and the rider broke into a clearing.

From the look of him, he was a Cossack. Silver cartridge cases glittered in the sun and the fur on his *kubanka* rippled in the wind. His horse was lathered, its eyes staring with exertion. The Cossack sent a hasty glance over his shoulder and applied his whip.

Whatever was following him did not break into the clearing. A rifle shot roared. The Cossack sat bolt upright as though he had been a compressed steel spring. His head went back, his hands jerked, and he slid off the horse, rolling when he hit the ground.

I remember his *kubanka* bounced and jumped and shot in under a bush. The horse zigzagged for a moment, slowed down and then stood with head drooping at the edge of the glade, too tired to eat.

Ordinarily I would not have injected myself into such a mess, but Ekaterinburg's reception had ruffled my temper and I knew that no Cossack would play in with the other side.

I pulled my rifle out of the saddle boot and waited, lying in the shadow of a big pine. Presently, three men came out of the forest, dismounted and looked down at the fallen rider.

They were shaggy brutes, those men, wearing dirty blouses and over-large black boots. They were armed with revolvers and rifles and knives. Veritable walking arsenals.

One of them aimed a kick at the dead Cossack's side. This was a cruel country and probably the Cossack would have done the same to his enemy, but the gesture squeezed my finger tight on the trigger.

The man stumbled with a startled grunt and sprawled in the grass, twisting about and holding his throat. The other two looked hurriedly about and, seeing nothing, made for their horses.

It was not my fight, but I knew that they would bring aid back with them. I put a snap shot into one's shoulder and missed the other completely in my anxiety to hit straight.

The one got away and I knew he would not be back for some little time—until he had collected a war party.

I went down to the three bodies. The Cossack's eyes were tightly closed, but when he heard me coming, he shot them wide and stared at me, rigid with pain. His sleek coat was dusty and blood was discoloring the gray cartridge cases.

Feebly, he motioned for me to come closer. I propped him up and a smile flickered across his ashy face. He had a small, arrogant mustache with waxed points. The blackness of it stood out strangely against the spreading pallor of death.

"The . . . *kubanka* . . . Gajda . . . "

That was all he would ever say. I laid him back into the soft grass and looked about for his hat. When I found it, it looked like a very ordinary hat to me. Nothing sewed into the band that I could find.

But he had been so anxious about it that I tucked it under my arm. I was going back to Gajda's outfit anyway.

But getting away with that hat was not going to be so easy. I had started up the slope to my horse when I heard the hammer of hoofs coming up. I sprinted forward and leaped into my saddle and sank in my spurs.

I swore loudly into the whipping wind. I had had no business getting into this fight in the first place. My duty was to get back to the main command and tell them that Ekaterinburg was strongly guarded. Now I had picked up the Cossack's torch. These others had killed the Cossack. What would happen to me?

For more than an hour I galloped through those sweet-smelling forests, choosing the thickest-foliaged road, trying to place distance between myself and those men from Ekaterinburg.

It's an ugly sensation, that of being hunted. Unable to gauge just how far you are from your harassers, you are in constant fear of being overhauled. You cannot look back every moment. You are afraid to breathe. Your heart comes up and beats in your throat and your nerves strain and tingle with the terror of it.

My horse had already had a hard ride. Now he began to stumble and his shaggy, mallet head sunk further down toward his knees. I pulled the rifle from its boot and slowed, looking expectantly back.

At first I could not believe that I was alone, but when the wooded slopes merely sighed in the wind and I could catch no glimpse of pursuit, I began to relax.

I gave the horse a breather and then went on with a saner pace, making my way between the big trees toward a path I knew would carry me on into camp. I still held the *kubanka*, not knowing that I carried an empire beneath my arm.

The wound I had thought a scratch began to ache. It was in the fleshy part of my left side, just under the armpit. The jouncing of the hard-seated horse made it hurt.

When I reached the path I heard a low whistle ahead of me. I stopped, still in the trees, wondering if I had run into another ambush. The whistle came again.

A man moved his horse out of the woods and into the trail, hailing me. It was an Englishman named Stone-Mead, part of the outfit. He was a youngster, but the war had made him very old. His khaki was immaculate and he rode like a subaltern on parade.

"Hallo, Stuart. What have you there?"

"A hat," I replied.

"It must be a very important hat, the way you're carrying it. You look like you've had a devilish hard run, man. Anything up?"

"Ekaterinburg is well manned," I said. "I'd better get the news through before some brass hat decides to attack it with a patrol."

"But what about the hat?"

"It must be very important. Three men have been killed because of it."

His smile hardened into wonder as he looked the *kubanka* over. "Nothing in it."

"I know, but a Cossack told me to take it to Gajda. Maybe Gajda will know more about it."

I must have looked very tired, as I had had a long ride and the wound was aching terribly. Stone-Mead looked at me for some time.

"See here, old fellow, you look about done in. I'm going back to command. Let me take the news and this hat, eh? There's a small hut over there and the peasant is pretty cordial to us. The Reds ran off all his horses, he tells me. You lie in there. It's too far back for you and my horse is fresh."

There was nothing wrong with the proposal. In fact, it was good judgment. The information was important. They had to know about Ekaterinburg. And a weary man does not keep a sharp lookout.

I gave him all the data and the *kubanka*, and he rode off down the trail, heading back toward command which was still many miles away. Then I went over to the hut.

The *mujik*, when he saw my khaki, was very cordial. He was an old fellow, bent up with rheumatism until he had to lean on a cane. His beard gave him the look of a patriarch, but his eyes reminded me of the Imperial Seal.

He had a small loft where he sometimes made a bed for visitors. He guided me there, brought me some meat on a tin platter and then left me to sleep.

I washed off the clotted blood and undid my first-aid kit and soon I was very comfortable, surrounded by the sweet hay. I must have dozed for a long time because it was dark when I awoke. Through cracks in the floor I saw the flicker of a candle below.

Men's voices came rumbling up into the loft. Heavy voices, full of threat. I pressed myself to the boards and watched and listened.

With a start I recognized the man I had missed that afternoon. About his waist was girded a Webley.

The owner of the place was crouched against the wall, watching silently. One of the strangers looked in his direction and spat, saying, "Tsarist!"

Then I almost cried out. Sitting in the exact center of the table was the Cossack's hat!

The Webley connected up instantly. Stone-Mead was dead.

"There is no message in it," said the man I recognized.

"But there might be. These *tsar* lovers are too smart, and we cannot allow anything to get through. Especially tonight. Those Czechs—"

"Ah, well," said another, seating himself at the unpainted table and scraping his boots on the floor. "Let us divide this while we can."

He pulled a roll of bills from his pocket. English pound notes, they were. Stone-Mead's money.

"What will we do with Ian's share?" said the man with the money.

"To hell with Ian. Let him rot out there. The wolves will clean him up. So much more for the rest of us."

"That Englishman shot straight," said the man with the money, and began to deal out the bills into rumpled piles. There was little money there, but it must have been a lot to these men. They greedily clutched it and stuffed it into their blouses.

Stone-Mead and Ian. Two more dead for that *kubanka*. Five in all. I stared moodily at the hat sitting like a round tower in the center of the table. It was black, the hue of death.

It must, I thought, be very, very important.

"What do you mean, tsarist," said the one with the Webley,

"by having a horse in your barn, eh? You had no horse yesterday. I was here and saw that you had none."

"I found it on the trail," said the old man, stubbornly.

"A likely excuse. How do you account for an American saddle blanket there?"

I froze to the planks. I heard chairs scrape and boots rap the floor.

"Perhaps he is in the loft."

"Perhaps," said the others. "You go up and see, Dmitri."

"I? Come, all of us will go."

My palm closed around the cold butt of the .45. I moved nearer the top of the ladder. The candle sent a flickering shadow into my range of vision. Dmitri and the rest were on their way.

Boots rasped on the ladder rungs. I slid off the safety and shoved the gun toward the edge. A cap came over the top.

Here was no case for niceties. I fired straight into the man's face. Smoke haze hung where the head had been. The body slammed back to the floor below.

The others shouted. Bullets smashed through the planks about me, and the splinters whined above the thunder of guns.

The old man yelled. I caught the odor of woodsmoke above the acrid stench of powder. Boots pounded again and a red light flickered up through the cracks. Light and heat. They had set the house on fire!

I jumped down the ladder. The old peasant was lying in a crushed heap against the wall, shot in the face. The *kubanka* was gone.

I fired straight into the man's face.

Swinging a shutter back, I jumped through the window and lit running. Riders were getting away. Flames shot through the roof of the hut and lit up the trail.

The range was not fifty feet although the garish flames made the shooting uncertain.

I fired at the last in line and dropped him. Another spun his mount about and tried to pot me. Running forward, completely amok, I fired straight up into his chest.

The trail was empty. The sparks were shooting a hundred feet in the air from the burning hut. I backed off from the heat.

Later I tried to find the *kubanka* but it was gone. Two men dead in the trail. Two men dead in the hut. Nine men had died for a hat. And I did not know why. It was July eighteenth.

For the next few weeks I spent most of my time getting well and keeping up with the slow advance upon Ekaterinburg. Gajda was in no great hurry. He was sparing his men, making sure of what he captured.

We were fighting steadily against the slowly withdrawing Reds. You heard vague rumors of it. Some fragmentary reports. But it did not figure greatly in history beside the big drums of the Western Front.

Nevertheless, men were dying by the hundreds. This was a fierce, ugly conflict, cruel and medieval. No quarter was given. The armies fought as had the armies of Genghis Khan. Cavalry against cavalry, hand-to-hand on foot. Bloody work, cruel work. And all so futile.

We were still hoping for the best, Kolchak and all the others wanted to set Russia back together. We all tried to plan the thing several ways to be sure, but in the back of our heads we were counting upon the *tsar*.

We took the town and its copper and gold mines. We drove them out and killed those who would not drive. We had reached Russia proper and the way looked open before us.

One night while I was doing some scouting through the town I happened into a small dive which had been reported Red. An American sergeant was with me, and when I went down the steps into the smoky, crowded room, he waited at the top.

I tried to make the call look unofficial, not wanting trouble if I could help it. I took my seat at a table against the wall and ordered a drink.

Looking about the room, I discovered that nearly all the men present were of the soldier type. They were dressed in castoff odds and ends of uniforms.

But one thing stood out in that crowd. A *kubanka*. The man that wore it looked vaguely familiar. It was possible that I had met him somewhere, as Ekaterinburg was a small place. But the thought persisted that this *kubanka* was *the kubanka*. The man was certainly not a Cossack and the hat was far better than his blouse.

I was on the point of making an investigation of the matter, when the man himself rose and came weaving down the room toward me.

Silence fell in the place. All eyes followed the man who approached me. Then everyone looked at me. Out of the corner of my eye I saw the sergeant unloosen his holster flap.

As slowly as I could, I placed my hand near my gun.

The man crouched forward, a yard from me, his black eyes angry. "Do not move, comrade. You are among my friends. I believe there is some small matter between us."

"If there is, I'm not aware of it."

He pulled a gun from his pocket. "Perhaps it would be better if you marched into the back room where we can talk."

I stood up, turning up my coat collar. The sergeant caught the signal. The roar of his .45 was deafening. The man before me clawed at a table and pulled it down with him.

Back against the wall, I watched the others surge up in black rage. The .45 fired again. I had my gun out, firing.

Suddenly they yelled at me to stop. Quiet settled on the place. Three men were down, huddled into themselves. My ears hurt from the sound of shots in those close confines.

They had no taste for death, those others. They did not know whether to face me or my sergeant at the top of the steps. I reached down and picked up the *kubanka* and walked through the men and up the steps and into the better-smelling night.

In the hotel we used for the staff, I sat down on the edge of the bed and began to take the *kubanka* apart. But before I had spent much time on it, I saw that the stitching of the brim was very bad.

With this as a clue, I called in a White Russian Intelligence man.

"See here," I said. "I want to know if you can make anything out of this stitching here?"

54

He examined it under the light and then began to smile. "It's Russian code. Wait, I'll translate it for you."

Presently, frowning and suddenly melancholy, he handed me a slip.

It said: "*Tsar* held at Ekaterinburg, house of Ipatiev. Will die July 18. Hurry."

That was the first clue we had of the death of Nicholas II and his family. We had not been aware of their presence in the town and they were certainly not there now.

We got to work. We questioned and searched. We found blood stains in the house of Ipatiev. We found some charred garments in the woods out of which fell several jewels which had evidently been sewn in the lining.

He had been shot with his family and the bodies had been buried, we supposed, in a peat bog nearby.

You see, the Cossack had been a tsarist messenger, and if that *kubanka* had gotten through, the *tsar* might have been saved by either threats or force.

This is the *kubanka*. I wish I could throw it away, but don't you think a dozen lives is too high a price for any hat?

Stuart rose and placed the *kubanka* at the other end of the room and reached for his pack of cards. But the rest of us were still thinking about the story. The stitching, as he had said, was done in long and short threads along the band and the presence of the thing was somehow ugly. It weighed upon us as had the day.

But after a bit we started to pitch the cards again. Stuart

sent one sailing down the room. It touched the brim and teetered there. Then, with a flicker of white, it coasted off the side and came to rest some distance away, face up.

We moved uneasily. I put my cards away.

The one Stuart had thrown, the one which had missed, was the king of spades.

Starch and Stripes

Starch and Stripes

CAPTAIN EDDIE EDWARDS of the *gendarmerie*, stationed in the hills back of Cape, had a hazy idea that senators did nothing more rash than shake their fists at each other on the senate floor. But he was wrong, though it was not until noon of that hot, sizzling hot, tropical day that he knew it. Senators were also vaguely responsible for appropriations to the Marine Corps, and Captain Eddie Edwards vaguely connected appropriations with his own punctual paycheck. He didn't know, that hot morning, that the weight of these same appropriations rested solely on his own meaty shoulders. Captain Eddie had other things to worry him.

The glorified highwayman they called "Charley" for short and who had a habit of upsetting the hills back of Cape was, Captain Eddie supposed, worry enough for one man. But he was wrong, and he didn't know it until the sun reached that unbearable zenith and kicked all shadow out of the back door.

Charley wasn't this "general's" right name, but it sounded like it somewhat, and Marines have a habit of perverting things in a direct climbing ratio of danger to humor.

Captain Eddie of the *gendarmerie* was just plain Gunnery Sergeant E. C. Edwards, USMC, but if they wanted to give him a flock of gooneys to command in the boondocks, and hand out pay and a half and the title of captain, it was all right with this leatherneck. They paid him well because his work was dangerous—the senators didn't think so, and that was one of the things they wanted to investigate.

Captain Eddie Edwards was sitting with his feet on the open shelf of his field desk. His campaign hat was pulled down over his eyes until it almost hid the square, bristly jaw. But he wasn't asleep. He shaded his eyes against the sunbeams which came through the ancient thatch overhead. He was far from asleep—he was waiting. Waiting for the news which was bound to come before night. His runners had brought him glad tidings and Captain Eddie had acted accordingly. In a moment that battered field phone would ring and Second Lieutenant Murphy, Sergeant Jim Murphy of the Corps, would bellow out that Charley was walking right down the trail into the carefully laid trap.

Charley didn't often come to town. But it seemed he had a lady friend he wanted to see in private, and as that lady friend was being paid good, hard cash by the *gendarmerie,* it was certain that the gooney "general" would walk into his reception—and with only a pair of bodyguards to keep him company. That was a break, according to Captain Eddie, because sniping had been going on, and the district was a hot, white flame under a whiter, hotter sun.

And then something roared out of the clouds and landed on the square parade ground. A helldiver, USMC painted with the globe and anchor on its side. And then something tall and straight was thundering through the rough untrimmed grass toward the headquarters shack. The something was Lieutenant Colonel Cramer, USMC.

GET 4 FREE BOOKS!

You can have the titles in the Stories from the Golden Age delivered to your door by signing up for the book club. Start today, and we'll send you **4 FREE BOOKS** (worth $39.80) as your reward.

—◦►—

The collection includes 80 volumes (book or audio) by master storyteller L. Ron Hubbard in the genres of science fiction, fantasy, mystery, adventure and western, originally penned for the pulp magazines of the 1930s and '40s.

—◦►—

YES! ☐

Sign me up for the Stories from the Golden Age Book Club and send me my first book for $9.95 with my **4 FREE BOOKS** (FREE shipping). I will pay only $9.95 each month for the subsequent titles in the series. Shipping is FREE and I can cancel any time I want to.

First Name _____ Middle Name _____ Last Name _____

Address _____

City _____ State _____ ZIP _____

Telephone _____ E-mail _____

Credit/Debit Card #: _____

Card ID# (last 3 or 4 digits): _____ Exp Date: _____ / _____

Date (month/day/year) _____ / _____ / _____

Signature: _____

Comments: _____

Check here ✓ to receive a FREE Stories from the Golden Age catalog
or go to: **GoldenAgeStories.com**.

Thank you!

"What the hell's the matter with you?" bellowed Cramer from the crazy rectangle of a door.

Captain Eddie clicked his heels and saluted and gave his surprise away by saying, "Yes, sir."

"Yes, sir, be damned!" roared Lieutenant Colonel Cramer. "This is the lousiest, most rundown pigpen I've soiled my boots on! Why the devil aren't you in uniform?"

As a matter of fact, Captain Eddie *was* in uniform, except for an unbuttoned shirt pocket and maybe a pair of non-regulation laced boots. And so he said nothing, but stood there respectfully, wondering where the lightning would strike next.

"You've got two hours to get this hole cleaned up. Two hours, understand? If it isn't, I'll bobtail you down to a buck rear rank."

Captain Eddie said, "Yes, sir. Would the colonel mind telling me what's up?" He was smarting under the injustice of the charge that his camp was dirty. Maybe it was, a little, but you couldn't set fifty men—gooneys at that—to cleaning and fighting all at the same time. What the hell did the colonel think this was, a model home for old soldiers? But Captain Eddie kept that to himself.

The officer from down at Cape was raising an unnecessary amount of dust by swishing his riding crop about. He scowled for the general effect and sat down in Captain Eddie's rickety chair.

"I tried to phone you," accused the colonel.

Captain Eddie gulped silently. He had cut off that line to connect up with the nearby village where Charley was about to be trapped. "Must be down, sir. Them gooneys are always cutting hell out of the line."

"Humph," said Cramer. "Now listen to me. Four senators and the general are coming up to inspect your camp. They'll be here between two and four by plane."

"Four . . . four . . . you mean that four senators are going to come up to this hole? Beggin' the colonel's pardon, sir, but they must be nuts!"

Cramer scowled, though he agreed with Captain Eddie perfectly. "I advised them to go down to Greenham's camp, but when I steered them clear of this place they wanted to come here immediately." It was a military lie, for the colonel had expressly advised the Edwards outfit—but then, praise is punk for soldiers.

"That boot!" gasped Captain Eddie. "But senators . . . senators and the general. . . . Don't them birds know that it's dangerous flying around here—or even standing around here? Why, right now, beggin' the colonel's pardon, some gooney might be takin' a bead on the colonel's left ear."

Before the colonel could stop himself, he felt of the ear and looked toward the door. The gesture made him soar into fine heights of military parlance.

"The appropriation is due for a vote next month. You wouldn't understand that, but it means that we either get what we need or we have to slice up all our corps. They're talking of laying off a couple thousand men and officers. Now pay attention. These four senators are the big guns on the Ways and Means Committee. They've been taking a cruise of the West Indies and inspecting our work. This post is their last stop. So far, they're doubtful as to the value of our work here." The colonel smashed his riding crop down among the papers and sent them flying. "By Montezuma's ghost, you've got to prove up. Understand?"

And then Captain Eddie of the *gendarmerie* remembered something which made him forget that colonels were colonels and that it was damned hot. He relaxed and leaned forward.

"My lord!" said Captain Eddie. "I'll have to recall my men from the town!"

"Certainly," rasped Cramer. "Did you expect to stand parade by yourself?"

"That ain't it! Charley—that bandit, I mean. He's coming in today. I've been waiting for the call. Murphy and a couple dozen are out there waiting for him now. They'll call any minute. This is a chance in a million."

Cramer knew all about the gooney "general" and how important that work was. He knew just what it meant to Captain Eddie Edwards and the district. But there were other things, such as compulsory retirement for lack of funds and the slicing up of the corps. And Cramer never changed his hand once he began to play it out.

"What of it?" bellowed the colonel. "You've had months to get him and you haven't. One day doesn't amount to a hill of beans. Call in your men." And then he saw something in Captain Eddie's eye which bordered on insubordination. Cramer's voice dropped to a parade-ground bawl. "And as for you—you're the dirtiest lout I ever laid my eyes on. You need a shave and you need a clean uniform. You'd better not let me catch you wearing those laced boots again, either. You're the most slovenly Marine I've seen for many a day."

Captain Eddie forgot to protest against the force of this onslaught. Something else had come up. This was his last partially clean uniform—and it was sweaty and very sour.

"If the colonel will excuse me, sir, I'd better be getting busy."

"I'll say you had. I don't want the whole corps to be wrecked just because you don't know the first thing about keeping up a post or even keeping yourself clean. Snap into it!"

Captain Eddie went away from there and left the colonel at his task of making hash out of paper with his riding crop.

A coal-black sergeant was jerked out of his comfortable doze with an onslaught which made him forget to salute. Captain Eddie's patois was never very good and now it was vile. The sergeant scurried away from there to bawl out a set of corporals who in turn would lace down innocent privates who in turn tonight would beat their wives.

Captain Eddie went into his sleeping hut and pulled his ebony swiper from his sleep against the wall. "Where the hell is my laundry?" Captain Eddie's voice was very dark and his jaw was very hard.

The boy knew that Captain Eddie knew that the laundry would not be sent until the morrow. But this was no time for protestations. Instead the boy took his verbal drubbing and went to work on Captain Eddie's best shoes.

The leatherneck looked into his locker trunk and started pulling blues, greens and khaki out by the handful. When he arrived at the bottom he found a moldy blouse and a pair of pants which had frayed cuffs. But they needed pressing and that very badly. They were limp for want of starch and they wouldn't stand up for ten minutes under this sun—yet upon them depended a very handsome set of gunnery sergeant's chevrons.

Captain Eddie put on his khaki helmet with its captain's stripes upside down. He buckled his well-oiled, carefully kept Colt against his thigh and called for his suitcase-size horse. While the horse was coming he made sure of his gun. You didn't go into the village these days unarmed. Some *caco* would take a crack at you if he knew he was safe from harm.

Satisfied that two squads were busily policing the parade ground and that others were cleaning equipment, Captain Eddie mounted and galloped down the trail. He usually spared his horse because all these horses were so small, but now he was thinking of chevrons and recalling Murphy and giving up the *caco* "general," and the pony caught all the consequences. Captain Eddie did not know which could be worse—senators or Charley. Both were now synonyms for oblivion.

Through a ragged gully, with his pony's hoofs sending rocks flying away from the red-clay trail, Captain Eddie caught sight of the village. It was a jumble of concrete and stucco, with once-red sheet-iron roofs, and once-white walls. The streets, even though the dry season was here, were slimy with mud and other things much worse. Children with rice tummies and running sores on their faces scampered into doorways. Wrinkled blacks who looked like witchdoctors, and probably were, sat placidly smoking and watched *"le capitaine de la gendarmerie"* pass by with unusual swiftness. Some of these were condescending enough to murmur, *"Bonjour, blanc,"* but the others remained discreetly silent. One never knew when a *caco* would be watching, and the price for friendliness with the *gendarmerie* was a very terrible thing.

Captain Eddie clattered east through the slimy foliage of a jungle trail until he was stopped by a hail from the brush. Upon hearing this he dismounted and threshed into view of the rear of a 1917 Light Browning, about which were clustered a waiting crew of gunners and the fly-bitten Lieutenant Murphy.

"Gawd's sake!" exclaimed Murphy, his red face growing redder. "You'd better be gettin' back to camp to lead the cutoff party in case Charley gets away." And he lurched up to his feet and stood with his hands on his hips and accusation on his face.

Sergeant Jim Murphy and Gunnery Sergeant Eddie Edwards had been through an awful lot together, and this was no time for observing the niceties of superiority.

"Button your trap," snapped Captain Eddie, looking very harassed but hard. "Fold up that toy cannon and get yourself back to camp. We got company."

"Company!" shrieked Murphy to the disdainful jungle. "Company! Who the blankety-blank-blank-blank cares about company? That black so-and-so will be along here *tout de suite* and if we miss him, who the hell is going to cut him off on the upper hill road? To hell with company."

"Forget Charley and start thinking about a starched shirt. You'd better or the stripes will be all over you and none on your sleeve. Double-time back to camp and take these gooneys with you!"

66

"You're nuts!" shouted Lieutenant Murphy. "Starched shirts, hooey! We've been waiting months for a crack at this damned *caco,* and I ain't giving it up for no starched shirt. What the blank-blank hell are we down here for if we don't get Charley? What . . ."

Captain Eddie knew how very mad he was himself and he didn't blame Lieutenant Murphy a plugged gourd's worth. But Captain Eddie looked even harder. "Scram. Four senators and the general are coming in two or three hours. Get that? Four senators are coming up here to inspect us by plane. The Cape colonel is waiting in my office now. Clean up that camp, police yourself and turn out the men. I ain't even got a clean shirt!"

Murphy looked like someone had just handed him a slug in the brisket. His jaw dropped and his color lightened. The *gendarmerie soldats* thought they had never seen him look so surprised or so sick. Generals and senators were all one and absolutely nothing to these lately barefoot boys.

"But . . ." stammered Lieutenant Murphy, "but I ain't got one either! Since that swiper stole my kit, I been short. I . . . oh, by all the blank-blank saints! It'll mean our commissions!"

"Worse than that," said Eddie, feeling judicial, "it'll mean the future of the corps. *En avant,* you black so-and-sos." He climbed back aboard his horse and headed back to town.

There was a certain whiskered lady who sometimes did washings very fast and who often proved her friendship for the *gendarmerie.* To her now went Captain Eddie, clothes under his arm. He went around to her back door, dismounted and stomped in.

"*Bonjour, blanc,*" said the black ebony antique. She was sitting down mending and chewing on something red, but at the sight of the harassed captain she dropped her work and came forward as swiftly as her two hundred and eighty pounds would allow.

"Iron these," said Captain Eddie. "Much starch, get it? Much starch and much smooth. Understand?"

"But yes. You have inspection now?"

Captain Eddie stared at her and said nothing.

"*Le général du cacos* will not be caught today? Because *le général du* Marines and politicians come today, *hein?*"

"How'd you know that?"

She shrugged and the gesture made her quiver beneath the damp clasp of the cheap, dirty gingham. "The drums speak little, tell much. They tell that *le général du cacos* comes this moment into the village."

Captain Eddie should have been used to it, but it happened so often that it was getting on his nerves. He took a step in the direction of the front door, but it opened before he could reach it and several young men and several dirty, naked children came tumbling in. Far up the street he heard the clatter of horses' hoofs. Perhaps three horses.

The rabble which had entered made themselves scarce at the back of the house, and now through all the town there was but one mar in the silence. Unshod hoofs coming serenely on, bearing the *caco* leader to his rendezvous with the dark lady—the queen of spades which could not now take the winning trick.

Suddenly Captain Eddie found out that he was very angry.

The audacity of the *caco* had gotten him, and the preceding events had been quite enough to frazzle him mentally.

"Listen," said Captain Eddie. "Take those clothes and fix them right away. Send them to camp in an hour."

"Name of God," breathed the black. "You . . ."

"Yes," snapped Captain Eddie, and went out of the back of the house.

The *caco* general, a glorified brigand at best, was highly in favor of the intervention of the United States. He never voiced it— Lord, no! He condemned all whites at the top of his voice and Marines in particular. He slaughtered, rather hideously with exquisite pain, any man who opposed him, Marines in particular. He held himself up as a Robin Hood, having read that book while in the States.

But without the armed intervention, the *caco* general would have been a general without a cause, and these do not win great favor. As long as he and the Marines or *gendarmerie* could fight, the general was a patriot and he could continue to gouge everyone. He had been haunting this particular district because of certain coffee tributes he found it worth his while to exact. If the Marines would only stay awhile, the general would be a very rich man indeed.

He rode now between two of his lieutenants who also called themselves generals when not in their mulatto leader's hearing. But he drowned them both in his elegance. They were as nothing compared to him. *Le général* was dressed in a white silk shirt which had leg-of-mutton sleeves. Lower extremities were encased in well-tailored riding breeches and better tailored boots. He was sprayed liberally with perfume.

However, his face was the finest point of all. His lips were so thin as to be no lips at all. His nose hinted at a very white father. His eyes were a sickly green shade that reminded one of a shark's belly six fathoms down.

The trio dismounted solemnly in front of the black queen's somewhat dilapidated shack and the two lieutenants needed no orders to know that they were to guard outside. They were not afraid of the *gendarmerie* today, if they ever were at all, for had they not heard the tale of those drums relayed all the way from Port? The Marine general, bah! The politicians, also bah! The *gendarmerie*—two bahs for their fumbling incompetence.

They never felt afraid of the Marine officers when they remembered that only fifty blacks were at the post and better than two thousand blacks were at the *caco* camp.

The general strode up the steps with a jingle of silver spurs and removed his hundred-dollar hat. He rapped stridently upon the door with his well-manicured right hand. He stepped away and waited imperiously for the door to open.

And then what must have been a vision to *le général* stood there. A slim, full-lipped girl with lustrous black hair. If she had not been so black, her skin would have been extraordinarily light in color, for it was obvious that something troubled her beyond all reason.

"Good day, my dear," said *le général,* smiling his handsomest. It was not until he had arranged his facial expression to his own liking that he saw that his adored was breathing somewhat rapidly. "What is wrong?"

"Nothing. It is but nothing. I am afraid, that is all. You come so bold in the bright sunlight. I am afraid the *gendarmerie* will see."

"*Pouf!*" said *le général,* looking very brave. "*Pouf!* for the *gendarmerie.*" It suited his taste for the dramatic not to tell her that the post was about to stand inspection and therefore would be fully occupied with its own affairs.

Though his bravery did not seem to steady the girl, she smiled and murmured, "Come in."

Le général went in amid his flashing silk and his jingling spurs. He carelessly threw that expensive hat to the floor and proceeded to gather the luscious queen into his slim arms. It was at this point that Captain Eddie made his entrance behind a leveled gat.

Captain Eddie's face was hard and set. His slate eyes were jets of toughness, and though he was somewhat soiled with his contact with the floor in back of the sofa, there was certainly nothing laughable about him.

And yet *le général* laughed. Softly and discreetly, but he laughed. He disentangled himself from the girl and gave her a thorough push which made her sit violently upon the complaining sofa. And then he stood back in the center of the room and looked at the threatening black tunnel of prospective oblivion and laughed again.

Captain Eddie didn't ask him what might be so funny. Captain Eddie was a Marine and a fighting man and he knew that tight spots sometimes got the best of your sense of humor. He merely waited for *le général* to stop that damned, almost silent cackling.

Captain Eddie moved himself from the back of the sofa and reposed his lean length against the wall.

"You are under arrest," he said.

Le général permitted himself to lessen his expression to a faint, superior smile.

"Not arrest," said *le général* in the best of Oxford English. "A prisoner of war."

"Have it any way you want, boy, but it won't make any difference when they put the hemp around your lemon-colored throat."

At that the *caco's* streak of humor went out as though drowned by a tropical rainstorm. His eyes went snaky and his hands began to inch up slowly.

On the couch where she had landed sat the queen of spades. The eyes of *le général* were upon her and the eyes were cold, stabbing things which went through her head and came out the back of her powdered neck. She shifted uncomfortably.

"He made me do it," she whimpered, dry-eyed. "He said he would shoot you when you opened the door if I did not." And this, of course, was merely a diplomatic lie which would save her something worse than torture later on at the hands of *le général's* men.

"Yes," said the general, his voice as silky and smooth as his shirt. "Pretty. Very pretty. You will die long before I, and I would not exactly care to match your death."

Her throat vibrated like a wind-whipped black sheet. Tiny beads of milky sweat stood out against her forehead through her powder. She knew that *le général du cacos* had just put the stamp on her death warrant and that not even the United States of America, the country which paid her so well, could save her. In short she was as good as a corpse and a mangled corpse at that.

Captain Eddie knew what she was thinking, but he did not look at her. He knew that it would be to his advantage to let *le général* take his own good time. The senators and his chief commanding officer were probably soaring in for a landing even now, but that couldn't be helped. He could still make it in time for the dress parade. Good old Murphy would take care of everything.

Le général was still giving the queen the eye and she was sitting up as though hypnotized—perhaps she was. And then Captain Eddie knew that he would have been better off watching the girl. He caught the faintest kind of a movement of her hand, but he caught it too late.

It was all one to the girl. She had the money and she would probably die unless she changed her coat. And change her coat she did. She could save face with *le général* and the *capitaine* would be dead, and she would still have the money.

Her dress was long and on the right leg she carried the dagger which most West Indian ladies carry there. Her hand went down, came up and her wrist flexed. Captain Eddie saw the dagger come and made the mistake of thinking it was intended for his heart. He moved his body but not his hand, and a numb, lukewarm pain told him he was skewered.

Before he could tighten his hold on the Colt, it was gone. He reached down quickly, but the hands of *le général* were even faster. The hand of *le général* was suddenly holding a Derringer.

73

Her hand went down, came up and her wrist flexed.
Captain Eddie saw the dagger come and made the mistake
of thinking it was intended for his heart.

One barrel spoke with its tongue of flame and the Colt went skidding away.

Le général was not laughing now. He was an icy pillar of vengeance. Through his lipless mouth he spat, "Back up quickly! Piérre, Loup! Come here!"

Captain Eddie backed up and pulled the knife out of the back of his hand. It had missed the bones and had gone all the way through. He said nothing as he watched the lieutenants enter and when he saw the queen of spades clutch beseechingly at *le général*'s left arm. Captain Eddie dropped the flimsy bit of steel to the floor. To use it he would commit nothing but suicide. He was a fighting man, Captain Eddie, and he knew when the ammunition was low, and he was enough of a gambler to realize when the ace in the deck was crimped.

Piérre and Loup tied him up with a rather unnecessary amount of vigor, and then Loup went away to bring the hundred men needed to escort him back into the hills where they could torture him at leisure. *Le général* was standing there watching him and trying to think up a few new ones.

"*La gendarmerie,* bah!" said *le général* and spat squarely and accurately at Captain Eddie's upturned face.

They put him in the back room amid the garbage the queen of spades had evidently forgotten to throw out into the street, and they left him there with blood running out of his hand and the smell of stale charcoal smoke in his nostrils—among other things—and for a time, at least, he was forgotten. The rope gag was cutting his lips as rope gags always do, but that was not the least of Captain Eddie's worries.

He was AWOLoose. Court-martial if he ever got back. He'd disobeyed the colonel's orders to forget Charley. He'd left his camp in turmoil just when the corps needed him the worst. When the senators of the Ways and Means Committee got there, they'd wonder where he was, and no matter how many lies that very capable Marine general would tell them, they'd know that everything was very slipshod and slovenly and that the corps wasn't worth appropriating for. The senators evidently hadn't thought so before, and they'd certainly be convinced of it now. Two thousand men out, morale shattered, Cramer retired with the others and all because Captain Eddie—no, Gunnery Sergeant Edwards—was lying here in a dirty kitchen smelling things not fit for the human nose. He felt very war-worn and weary.

To say that Captain Eddie did not know fear would be a deliberate lie. All men who have any bravery at all know fear but are strong enough to overwhelm it before it paralyzes them. Besides, there were certain things which had happened in his district which should have made him die on the spot from stark fright.

Le général, according to his own statement, was a gentleman. He had been trained in France for law work. He had had the best advantages the civilized world could offer. Once he had run for the presidency. Notwithstanding, *le général* was the most accomplished master of bestial cruelty in the realm.

Orgies of torture were his chief indulgence. That month he had found a Marine private carrying a dispatch up from Cape, and when Captain Eddie had arrived at the scene, the leatherneck had been stripped, piece by piece, of all his flesh.

He had been picked clean by knives in human, or inhuman, hands, but his skeleton still lived in agony. What Captain Eddie had done out of mercy would never go on record. *Le général* had thought his work so fine that he had broadcast its narrative via the drums to all the nation.

And Captain Eddie, lying there in the scattered garbage, remembered the two white engineers who had been stripped and lashed down on anthills. *Le général* had had no quarrel with them, but they had died. Captain Eddie wondered if the ratio would increase—for he had caused *le général* no little worry.

The passing time had lost significance when Captain Eddie heard a sound which made him groan aloud. Not more than a block away horses with steel-shod hoofs were trotting. Only one group of ponies in all this district wore shoes—*la gendarmerie*. And Captain Eddie groaned, not because there was a possibility of his rescue, but because it was evident that Murphy had said to hell with the senators and the staff and had gone off to locate his commanding officer.

On the tail of that thought came the words of Murphy. The Marine thought he talked low-voiced, but he was easily heard for two blocks. "It ain't no use lookin' around here. They've taken him to the hills."

A slinking black came through the kitchen door and Piérre, rifle in hand, his sweat-greased black face alive with cruelty, went to the glassless window and started to draw a bead on Murphy. Captain Eddie tried to cry out through his gag in warning, but the hemp only gashed him deeper. Piérre's fingers were closing over the trigger guard.

But Piérre was not quite the soldier he thought himself to

be, and Murphy's alert gray eyes were looking for just such a move—so common in the village. A .45 bellowed through the heat and the *caco* jumped back as though pulled by a string. Before he hit the floor he was dead, betrayed by the sun on his rifle barrel.

Captain Eddie lost no time. It was not likely that Murphy would follow up his own shot, and the machete at Piérre's side was beckoning. Captain Eddie's tied hands went around the hilt and the three-foot knife with its light-sharp edge slithered free and darted down to the leg bonds. An instant's work and those were off. Reversing the knife in his hands, he slashed away at his wrists. He was not thinking about his luck, for this shooting a *caco* in the village before the *caco* tried to get you was age-old to the Marines.

Boot beats were coming from the front room, heralding the approach of *le général*. All the warning he had had consisted of a pistol shot in the street, and it was not enough. And so *le général* walked straight into the muzzle of Piérre's Russian Army rifle, at whose business end stood the very untidy late captive. *Le général* paused, but before Captain Eddie could utter a word, the *caco* had dived for him.

But Captain Eddie didn't shoot. Nothing so nice as that for Charley. Charley would have to pay for that Marine private, those engineers and better than a score of others. And so the Marine merely avoided the rush and waded in with his fists.

He was stiff and aching from the rope, but when he knew he had to do a thing, he did it. He forced *le général* down into the garbage and sat on his rage-quivering stomach.

Charley raved in two languages and fought with the wiles of three races. He raised himself up and strove to throw off his assailant. Captain Eddie held him, and when the *caco* reached for his Derringer, Captain Eddie was forced to the last expedient of laying the *caco* out with a sock on the jaw.

Le général sagged and lay still. He was plastered from head to foot with the filth into which he had first thrown the Marine; his appearance now, if one felt like laughing, was laughable.

Feeling that he'd done a very swift and very neat job, Captain Eddie recovered his Colt from *le général*'s belt and went out to find the queen of spades—but she was gone. In her place was the sound of coming horses, many of them. Loup was returning with the men who were to take the Marine back to camp.

In a quarter second, Captain Eddie had made a decision and within a minute it had been carried out. It was rather difficult to get the silk shirt over *le général*'s wrists, but it was done. Captain Eddie thought twice before he donned *le general*'s pants, but he did so. And the Marine was quite disgusted when he was forced to dress *le general* in the uniform of the *gendarmerie*. However, it was all for the best.

Surveying himself in the mirror, Captain Eddie decided that he was neither too light of skin nor too meaty of body. And when he had liberally patted the queen of spades' powder over the *caco*'s lemon-colored face, *le général* at least looked white.

Out back were three horses, and the *caco* was loaded

aboard the *gendarmerie* mount and showed signs of returning consciousness. Captain Eddie mounted the silver-inlaid saddle of the *caco* and showed him the pistol in his hand.

"Ride!" said Eddie. "Hard, and straight for the *gendarmerie* camp. Otherwise I'll puncture your tires for you."

Le général rode, for there was nothing else he could do. He was rather appalled at the thought of himself in the *gendarmerie* uniform, for he had heard the sound of his own horses and he knew that the first shots would arrive in the back of the khaki shirt. And so *le général* rounded the back of the dilapidated shack like a hurricane and streaked out toward the trail of the *gendarmerie,* his khaki rags flying. Close at his heels, without a single backward glance, and trying to make it appear that he chased his effigy, Captain Eddie was coming on hoofs which rolled like kettle drums.

The *cacos* stared in great surprise at the retreating pair. And then they applied their spurs and a hundred miniature ponies scattered away in pursuit. They would help *le général* catch *le capitaine.*

The pair raced through the ravine and came out on the plain. They lanced through the boughs of thorn trees—which did their clothes little good—and hurdled scraggly cactus. Red clay rose up from their hoofs and spattered them. *Le général* rode like a man possessed of devils. No one knew better than he that his back would be the first target.

Ahead a rectangle of huts and trees were looming, and when they thundered near, *caco* pursuit stopping far behind, Captain Eddie knew the worst. The senators and the Marine general were already there and had rather more than started on their inspection of the black soldiers drawn up in company front. Captain Eddie saw ill-fitting duck suits and well-tailored khaki. He saw the hue of the Marine general's face and he knew that the worst was about to arrive.

The sentries at the gate raised rifles to port and bade the horsemen stop. They were unduly surprised to see the *caco* dressed as he was, and they were hard put to straighten out their black grins when they recognized their superior officer, Captain Eddie, in a white silk shirt, plastered with mud and torn at that.

"Take this man in charge!" snapped Captain Eddie, and when the sentries had done so, he swirled on out into the parade ground and flung himself away from his lathered pony. The *caco* spurs jingled and the remnants of the shirt flapped, and the Marine general looked more surprised than he ever had before in his life. The Marine general's capable hand came away from his Colt when he saw that he did not face the famed *caco*.

Lieutenant Colonel Cramer sought vainly to steer the four influential, but fat and perspiring, senators to the other end of the camp. But they had seen and their orator's jaws were sagging in their folds of flesh.

Captain Eddie saluted. "Beggin' the general's pardon, sir, but I got detained." Out of the corner of his eye he saw the men grinning and saw that Murphy was looking straight ahead like a good soldier, though dressed like a very sloppy boot.

"Huh!" roared the general. "So you got detained. I send express orders for you to prepare this camp for inspection, and you allow yourself to be detained. You know what this means?"

"Yes, sir," said the miserable Eddie, swallowing hard.

"It means you'll be relieved of this command and bobtailed down to a buck. It means," and here the great Marine forgot all about the senators in back of him and gave way to all the bitterness within him—if this had gone well he would not have been retired.

"It means that the Corps is going to be slashed to bits. It means that you and all the rest of us are going to be out on our blank-blank ears. You've gummed up the works! I never saw such blank-blank-blank slovenliness as this camp. And what the blank-blank-blank hell do you mean reporting out of uniform?"

Captain Eddie found voice. "Beggin' the general's pardon, sir, but the *caco* general . . ."

"To hell with the *caco* general! You've disobeyed orders, and if you don't know what that means, you're going to find out. You haven't even the courtesy to report to me in a decent uniform! What do you think this is? A masquerade?"

"But, General . . ."

"But, hell!" The great Marine's face was red and his crop bit furrows into his carefully polished boots. He was fast arriving at that sad state of anger where one loses all one's words.

However, the commanding officer was spared further effort by the advance of a rather heavily setup man in sweaty whites. It was one of the senators, Gregg by name.

Captain Eddie felt himself wilt. He knew what this man would say. He knew that the appropriation which was so vital was dead right here and now. Captain Eddie knew he had failed.

"Perhaps," rumbled Gregg, "this officer had some important work which we interrupted."

"I'm no officer, sir," said Captain Eddie. "I'm Gunnery Sergeant Edwards, serving with the *gendarmerie*."

"Thank you," said Gregg, smiling. "But according to the bill we put through to cover this, you have all the privileges of an officer. Tell me, Captain, what detained you."

"This guy Charley—I mean the *caco* leader. I had a trap set for him, sir, and he walked right into it. But I got word from Lieutenant Colonel Cramer, sir, that you were coming and I had to drop my plans. I'd been working on this for months, sir. This *caco* general has been killing Marines and terrorizing the country. He says he's a great patriot, but . . . "

"I know that," said Gregg. "What happened?"

"I captured him when he went to his girl's house. I swapped uniforms with him so I could get him away. He's that fellow down there by the gate in the ragged khaki."

The Marine general started to bellow something about the capture not making any difference, but Gregg stopped him.

"We'll talk to the *caco* leader in a little while. Right now, I have something to say."

Captain Eddie's silk-enclosed heart was down in the region of the silver spurs. This was the end, even though this senator looked like a regular after all.

"I've been to many of your posts around the Caribbean," said Gregg, "and I've seen some of the finest dress parades possible. Isn't that right, gentlemen?" He saw the other three nod sweaty foreheads and then went on. "We've met a lot of fine men who were drawing good pay to stay around and wait until they could give us dress parades. That is all I have seen. I was thoroughly convinced with my colleagues that your position here was sham. We were ready to strike out your portion of the appropriations bill."

The Marine general gave Eddie a nasty glare and then looked apprehensively at Gregg.

"But today," Gregg continued, "I see Marines at work for the first time. In spite of the consequences awaiting this man should he fail, he went on single-handed and captured the *caco* general. That called for courage of the highest order, and that you can't deny. I see that you are doing something here. For weeks I have waited to see what you could do. I see now.

"And this is what I advise." He stopped impressively and looked around him. "I will double the appropriation if you will make all the police work of this island in accordance with the experience of the *gendarmerie,* and that you place men such as Captain Edwards here in charge—in complete charge of the work. They alone understand. Do I make myself clear, General?"

The great Marine nodded, somewhat dazed.

"Less gold braid and more work. Fewer parades and more patrols. Do that and I will double the appropriation. Now let us go down and talk to the *caco* leader."

The group walked away and left the Marine general solemnly shaking Captain Eddie by the hand.

Story Preview

Story Preview

NOW that you've just ventured through some of the captivating tales in the Stories from the Golden Age collection by L. Ron Hubbard, turn the page and enjoy a preview of *Hurricane*. Join Captain Spar, who is wrongfully imprisoned on Devil's Island but makes a daring escape to the small island of Martinique—trailing his nemesis, the infamous Saint.

Hurricane

HE came through the rain-buffeted darkness, slipping silently along a wall, avoiding the triangular patches of light. His stealth was second nature because he had lived with stealth so long. And who knew but what death walked with him into the leaden gusts which swept through the streets of Fort-de-France, Martinique?

He was big, heavy boned, and he had once weighed more than he did. His eyes were silver gray, almost luminous in the night like a wolf's. His black hair was plastered down on his forehead, his shirt was dark, soggy with the tempest, and at his waist there gleamed a giant brass buckle. Capless and gaunt, feeling his way through the sullen city, he heard voices issuing from behind a door.

He stopped and then, indecisively, studied the entrance. Finally he rapped. A moment later a dark, fat face appeared in the lighted crack.

"*Qu'est-ce que c'est?*"

"I want food. Food and perhaps information."

"The police have forbidden us to open so late. Do you wish to cause my arrest?"

"I have money."

The doors opened wider. The mestizo closed and bolted

the double door. A half a dozen men looked up, curiously, and then returned to their rum punch.

"Your name is Henri," said the tall one, standing in a puddle of water which oozed out away from his shoes.

Henri raised his brows and rubbed his hands, looking up and down the tall one's height. "You know my name? And I know you. You are the one they call Captain Spar."

"Yes, that's it. Then you got the letter?"

"Yes, I received the letter. I do not often associate with . . . convicts."

Captain Spar made no move. "I have money."

"How much?"

"One hundred dollars."

Henri waved his fat hands. "It is not enough. There are police!"

"I have one hundred dollars, that's all."

"I expose no risk for a hundred dollars. Am I a fool? Go quickly before I call the *gendarmes*."

"I'll attend to getting out of here by myself. I want only food, perhaps some clothes."

Henri subsided. "But how did you come here?"

"Stowaway. The captain found me, allowed me to get ashore here, would carry me no further. Our friend wrote you in case that happened."

"He did not say that you would only have a hundred dollars. Let me tell you, young fellow, an American is conspicuous here on a black island. I run no risks for a paltry hundred dollars. If you are caught, you will be sent back and I will be sent with you. I disclaim any interest in you or knowledge of you. If you want food, I will serve it to you as a customer. That is all."

Henri waddled away, his neck sticking like a stump out of his collarless white-and-blue striped, sweat-stained shirt. Henri was greasy to a fault, thought Captain Spar. Slippery, in fact.

Presently Henri came back, bringing the makings of a rum punch—syrup, *rhum vieux*, limes and a bowl of cracked ice. Captain Spar made his own drink and as he sipped it, he said, "Would you know of a man here who calls himself the Saint?"

Henri shook his head. "Who is that? Can it be that you actually came back into French territory, risking your neck, to find a man?"

"Perhaps."

"Perhaps for some of that hundred—"

"If your information is right, you get paid."

"Tell me what you know of this man, first. Tell me why you want him."

Captain Spar looked over the glass rim and then nodded. "All right. You know my name. That's my right name, strangely enough. One time, not five years ago, it was a very respected thing, but now . . .

"Five years ago I was in Paramaribo, temporarily out of a job. I was approached by a ship's broker who said that a man who called himself the Saint was in need of a captain. I had not heard of the Saint, but it was said that his headquarters were Martinique.

"The job was simple enough. I was to sail for New York in command of a two-thousand-ton tub of rust. The loading had already been done, so they said. All I had to do was get aboard and shove off.

"Just as I was about to sail, men swarmed down upon the ship, boarded us, announced that they were police, and began to search. In a few minutes they had dragged a dozen men from the hold. They turned all of us over to the French authorities who immediately sent us down to French Guiana.

"I was accused of trying to aid penal colony convicts to escape, and with a somewhat rare humor, they determined that I should join the men they thought my comrades at their labor in the swamps.

"That was five years ago. Two weeks ago I made my way to the sea, found this friend of mine, recovered the money he had been keeping for me, stowed on a freighter, and here I am in Martinique. I want the Saint."

Henri nodded thoughtfully. "Yes, there is a Saint here."

Captain Spar sat forward, his sunken eyes lighting up with a swift ferocity. "Here? Where?"

"I can tell you all about it," said Henri, "but I do not want money for my efforts. Oh, no, *m'sieu*. You can do me a small favor, and then perhaps I shall tell you all about the Saint, where he can be found, how you can kill him."

"Name the favor," said Spar.

To find out more about *Hurricane* and how you can obtain your copy, go to www.goldenagestories.com.

Glossary

Glossary

STORIES FROM THE GOLDEN AGE *reflect the words and expressions used in the 1930s and 1940s, adding unique flavor and authenticity to the tales. While a character's speech may often reflect regional origins, it also can convey attitudes common in the day. So that readers can better grasp such cultural and historical terms, uncommon words or expressions of the era, the following glossary has been provided.*

ace of, within an: within a narrow margin of; close to.

Alexander the Great: king of Macedonia (an ancient kingdom, now a region in northern Greece, southwestern Bulgaria and the Republic of Macedonia) 336–323 BC, and conqueror of Greece and the Persian Empire (an ancient empire in western and southwestern Asia).

AWOLoose: AWOL; absent without leave, used to designate those who were gone for a relatively short time, as opposed to permanent deserters. At first AWOL was pronounced letter by letter. This is evident in the humorous World War I variant AWOLoose, meaning the same thing as AWOL. By the start of World War II, however, the pronunciation had changed to AY-wall, as if the initials constituted one word rather than an abbreviation. Humorously contrived attributions of the letters in World War II included "A Wolf On the Loose" and "After Women Or Liquor."

baleful: threatening (or seeming to threaten) harm or misfortune.

Baluchi: an eastern Iranian language spoken in Baluchistan.

Baluchistan: former territory of west British India, now the largest province in Pakistan. It is a mountainous region bordering on the Arabian Sea.

bobtail to a buck rear-rank: reduce to the lowest rank of private and to the rear or last in order of a body of troops.

bonjour, blanc: (French) hello, white man.

boot: a Marine or Navy recruit in basic training.

brawny: having physical strength and weight; rugged and powerful.

brigand: one who lives by plunder; a bandit.

burnoose: a long hooded cloak worn by some Arabs.

cabin job: an airplane that has an enclosed section where passengers can sit or cargo is stored.

caco: (French) a member of loosely knit bandit organizations who hired out to the highest bidder. Transfer of power in Haiti traditionally occurred when a political contender raised a *caco* army and marched on the capital. Transfer of power was completed when the incumbent fled the country with part of the treasury.

campaign hat: a felt hat with a broad stiff brim and four dents in the crown, formerly worn by personnel in the US Army and Marine Corps.

Cape: Cap-Haïtien; a city on the north coast of Haiti facing the Atlantic Ocean.

Colt: an automatic pistol manufactured by the Colt Firearms Company, founded in 1847 by Samuel Colt (1814–1862) who revolutionized the firearms industry with his inventions.

Cossack: a member of a people of southern European Russia and adjacent parts of Asia, noted as cavalrymen, especially during tsarist times. Their uniform coat had silver cartridges lined across the chest. Each cartridge contained enough gunpowder for one shot of their muzzle-loaded gun

crate: an airplane.

Cyrus the Great: the King of Persia (an ancient empire in western and southwestern Asia) and founder of the Persian Empire.

Czech: people of Czechoslovakia, a country in Central Europe (now called the Czech Republic). The Czech lands were under Habsburg rule (Austrian Empire) from 1526, later becoming part of the Austrian Empire and Austria-Hungary. The independent republic of Czechoslovakia was created in 1918, following the collapse of the Austro-Hungarian Empire after World War I.

Dehwar: a member of a tribe in the Baluchistan province of Pakistan.

Derringer: a pocket-sized, short-barreled, large-caliber pistol. Named for the US gunsmith Henry Deringer (1786–1868), who designed it.

devil-may-care: wildly reckless.

dickens: a severe reprimand.

drop on, got the: have achieved a distinct advantage over.

dry: indifferent, cold, unemotional.

Ekaterinburg: a city in the Russian Federation of Asia, in the Ural Mountains.

en avant: (French) forward.

flags or **flagstone:** a flat stone or stones used especially for paving.

Fort-de-France: the capital and largest city of Martinique, on the western coast of the island.

forty-five or **.45:** a handgun chambered to fire a .45-caliber cartridge.

French Guiana: a French colony of northeast South America on the Atlantic Ocean, established in the nineteenth century and known for its penal colonies (now closed). Cayenne is the capital and the largest city.

Gajda: Radola Gajda (1892–1948); a Czech military commander and politician.

gat: a gun.

gendarme: a police officer in any of several European countries, especially a French police officer.

gendarmerie: (French) a military body charged with police duties among civilian populations. The Haitian *gendarmerie,* organized in 1916, initially consisted of 250 officers and 2,500 men, to provide police services throughout the country. The *gendarmerie* was officered by Marine Corps personnel, most of whom were sergeants with officer rank in the Haitian service. The *gendarmerie* fought alongside Marine occupying forces during the *caco* wars.

Genghis Khan: (1162?–1227) Mongol conqueror who founded the largest land empire in history and whose armies, known for their use of terror, conquered many territories and slaughtered the populations of entire cities.

glacial: extremely cold.

G-men: government men; agents of the Federal Bureau of Investigation.

Great Bear Lake: freshwater lake in Canada's Northwest Territories, lying astride the Arctic Circle.

hein?: (French) eh?

helldiver: an American aircraft carrier-based dive bomber produced for the US Navy during World War II by the Curtiss-Wright Corporation, once a leading aircraft manufacturer of the United States.

highwayman: a person who robs on a public road; a thief.

Hopi: a Pueblo Indian people of northeast Arizona noted for their craftsmanship in basketry, pottery, silverwork and weaving.

hoplite: a heavily armored foot soldier.

house of Ipatiev: Ipatiev House; a merchant's house in Ekaterinburg where the former Emperor Nicholas II of Russia and several members of his family and household were executed. The house was demolished in 1977 and the magnificent "Church on the Blood," with many auxiliary chapels and belfries, was built there after the fall of the Soviet Union.

Imperial Seal: Imperial Seal of China; a seal carved out of a historically famous piece of jade.

Iskander of the Two Horns: Alexander the Great. He is also known in Eastern traditions as Dhul-Qarnayn (the two-horned one) because an image minted during his rule seemed to depict him with the two ram's horns of the Egyptian god Ammon.

Kolchak: Aleksandr Kolchak (1874–1920); a Russian naval commander and later head of part of the anti-Bolshevik forces during the Russian Civil War.

kubanka: a hat worn by Imperial Russian soldiers consisting of a wide band of black sheep wool with a flat top.

leatherneck: a member of the US Marine Corps. The phrase comes from the early days of the Marine Corps when enlisted men were given strips of leather to wear around their necks. The popular concept was that the leather protected the neck from a saber slash, though it was actually used to keep the Marines from slouching in uniform by forcing them to keep their heads up.

le capitaine de la gendarmerie: (French) the captain of the *gendarmerie.*

le général du cacos: (French) the general of the *cacos.*

legionnaire: a member of a legion; in Roman history a military division varying at times from 3,000 to 6,000 foot soldiers, with additional cavalrymen.

leg-of-mutton sleeves: sleeves that are extremely wide over the upper arm and narrow from the elbow to the wrist.

Light Browning, 1917: a light machine gun weighing fifteen pounds. It looks like and can be fired like an ordinary rifle, either from the shoulder or the hip. It was invented by John M. Browning (1855–1926), an American firearms designer.

Macedonian: someone from an ancient kingdom in northern Greece, where Alexander the Great created a vast empire.

mags: magnetos; small ignition system devices that use permanent magnets to generate a spark in internal combustion engines, especially in marine and aircraft engines.

Makran: the southern region of Baluchistan in Iran and Pakistan along the coast of the Arabian Sea.

mestizo: a racially mixed person, especially in Latin America, of American Indian and European (usually Spanish or Portuguese) ancestry.

Montezuma: an Aztec emperor of the sixteenth century.

mujik: (Russian) in tsarist Russia, a peasant.

nailing (me) down: variation of "pin down," meaning to prevent somebody from going anywhere.

Nicholas II: Nicholas II of Russia (1868–1918); last Emperor of Russia, King of Poland and Grand Duke of Finland. He ruled from 1894 until his forced abdication in 1917. Nicholas proved unable to manage a country in political turmoil and command its army in World War I. His rule ended with the Russian Revolution of 1917, after which he and his family were executed by Bolsheviks in July 1918.

Paramaribo: the capital and largest city of Dutch Guiana (now Suriname) in northern South America on the Atlantic Ocean.

Pasni: a fishing village on the coast of the Baluchistan province in Pakistan.

patois: a regional form of a language, especially of French, differing from the standard, literary form of the language.

percolate: to show activity, movement or life.

Port: Port-au-Prince; the capital and largest city of Haiti.

Punjab: a former province in northwest British India, now divided between India and Pakistan.

punk: worthless.

quarter: mercy or indulgence, especially as shown in sparing a life and accepting the surrender of a vanquished enemy.

Qu'est-ce que c'est: (French) What is that?

Ras el Kuh: a town located on the southern coast of Iran.

Ras Malan: a mountain in Baluchistan (southwestern Pakistan), which slopes into the Arabian Sea.

Reds: political radicals or revolutionaries who incite or endorse sweeping social or political reform, especially by the use of force, as a member of the Russian Social Democratic party that favored revolutionary tactics to achieve full socialization and seized supreme power in Russia during the Revolution (1917–1920) for the purpose of setting up a workers' state.

rhum vieux: (French) aged rum; rum that has aged at least three years.

Scheherazade: the female narrator of *The Arabian Nights,* who during one thousand and one adventurous nights saved her life by entertaining her husband, the king, with stories.

scourge: somebody or something that is perceived as an agent of punishment, destruction or severe criticism.

Semiramis: a mythical queen of Assyria (an ancient empire and civilization in western Asia) who is reputed to have conquered many lands.

shoot landings: pilot's lingo for the process of preparing a landing.

Siberia: an extensive region in what is now the Russian Federation in northern Asia, extending from the Ural Mountains to the Pacific.

soldats: (French) soldiers.

Sverdlovsk: a Russian city in the Ural Mountains, called Ekaterinburg from 1723 to 1924. Named Sverdlovsk until 1991 when it returned to its original name.

swiper: groom; a male servant who takes care of a man's clothes.

Tajik: someone living mainly in Tajikistan (a republic in central Asia), as well as parts of Afghanistan and China.

Teheran: the capital of Iran.

Tommies: common soldiers in the British Army; the term was most popularly used during World War I where German, French and Commonwealth soldiers referred to the British soldiers as *Tommies.*

tout de suite: (French) right away.

tsar: (Russian, also tzar) shortened form of *tsesar,* from Latin, *Caesar;* a male monarch or emperor, especially one of the emperors who ruled Russia until the revolution of 1917.

tsarevich: (Russian) son of a *tsar.* Nicholas II had a son, Alexei (1904–1918).

tsarist: an adherent of a *tsar,* a male monarch or emperor.

Urals: Ural Mountains; a mountain range in what is now the Russian Federation, extending north and south from the Arctic Ocean to near the Caspian Sea, forming a natural boundary between Europe and Asia.

USMC: United States Marine Corps.

Webley: Webley and Scott handgun; an arms manufacturer based in England that produced handguns since 1834. Webley is famous for the revolvers and automatic pistols it supplied to the British Empire's military, particularly the British Army, from 1887 through both World War I and World War II.

Western Front: term used during World War I and II to describe the "contested armed frontier" (otherwise known as "the front") between lands controlled by the Germans to the East and the Allies to the West. In World War I, both sides dug in along a meandering line of fortified trenches stretching from the coast of the North Sea, southward to the Swiss border that was the Western Front. This line remained essentially unchanged for most of the war. In 1918 the relentless advance of the Allied armies persuaded the German commanders that defeat was inevitable and the government was forced to request armistice.

West Indies: a group of islands in the North Atlantic between North and South America, comprising the Greater Antilles, the Lesser Antilles and the Bahamas.

White Russian or **White:** a person who is in opposition to a radical or revolutionary policy or doctrine. As a Russian who fought against the Bolsheviks (Russian Social Democratic party) in the Russian Revolution (1917–1920).

Yanks: Yankees; term used to refer to Americans in general.

L. Ron Hubbard
in the Golden Age
of Pulp Fiction

*In writing an adventure story
a writer has to know that he is adventuring
for a lot of people who cannot.
The writer has to take them here and there
about the globe and show them
excitement and love and realism.
As long as that writer is living the part of an
adventurer when he is hammering
the keys, he is succeeding with his story.*

*Adventuring is a state of mind.
If you adventure through life, you have a
good chance to be a success on paper.*

*Adventure doesn't mean globe-trotting,
exactly, and it doesn't mean great deeds.
Adventuring is like art.
You have to live it to make it real.*

— *L. RON HUBBARD*

L. Ron Hubbard
and American
Pulp Fiction

B ORN March 13, 1911, L. Ron Hubbard lived a life at
least as expansive as the stories with which he enthralled
a hundred million readers through a fifty-year career.

Originally hailing from Tilden, Nebraska, he spent his
formative years in a classically rugged Montana, replete with
the cowpunchers, lawmen and desperadoes who would later
people his Wild West adventures. And lest anyone imagine
those adventures were drawn from vicarious experience, he
was not only breaking broncs at a tender age, he was also
among the few whites ever admitted into Blackfoot society
as a bona fide blood brother. While if only to round out an
otherwise rough and tumble youth, his mother was that rarity
of her time—a thoroughly educated woman—who introduced
her son to the classics of Occidental literature even before
his seventh birthday.

But as any dedicated L. Ron Hubbard reader will attest, his
world extended far beyond Montana. In point of fact, and as the
son of a United States naval officer, by the age of eighteen he
had traveled over a quarter of a million miles. Included therein
were three Pacific crossings to a then still mysterious Asia, where
he ran with the likes of Her British Majesty's agent-in-place

L. Ron Hubbard, left, at Congressional Airport, Washington, DC, 1931, with members of George Washington University flying club.

for North China, and the last in the line of Royal Magicians from the court of Kublai Khan. For the record, L. Ron Hubbard was also among the first Westerners to gain admittance to forbidden Tibetan monasteries below Manchuria, and his photographs of China's Great Wall long graced American geography texts.

Upon his return to the United States and a hasty completion of his interrupted high school education, the young Ron Hubbard entered George Washington University. There, as fans of his aerial adventures may have heard, he earned his wings as a pioneering barnstormer at the dawn of American aviation. He also earned a place in free-flight record books for the longest sustained flight above Chicago. Moreover, as a roving reporter for *Sportsman Pilot* (featuring his first professionally penned articles), he further helped inspire a generation of pilots who would take America to world airpower.

Immediately beyond his sophomore year, Ron embarked on the first of his famed ethnological expeditions, initially to then untrammeled Caribbean shores (descriptions of which would later fill a whole series of West Indies mystery-thrillers). That the Puerto Rican interior would also figure into the future of Ron Hubbard stories was likewise no accident. For in addition to cultural studies of the island, a 1932–33

LRH expedition is rightly remembered as conducting the first complete mineralogical survey of a Puerto Rico under United States jurisdiction.

There was many another adventure along this vein: As a lifetime member of the famed Explorers Club, L. Ron Hubbard charted North Pacific waters with the first shipboard radio direction finder, and so pioneered a long-range navigation system universally employed until the late twentieth century. While not to put too fine an edge on it, he also held a rare Master Mariner's license to pilot any vessel, of any tonnage in any ocean.

Yet lest we stray too far afield, there is an LRH note at this juncture in his saga, and it reads in part:

"I started out writing for the pulps, writing the best I knew, writing for every mag on the stands, slanting as well as I could."

To which one might add: His earliest submissions date from the

Capt. L. Ron Hubbard in Ketchikan, Alaska, 1940, on his Alaskan Radio Experimental Expedition, the first of three voyages conducted under the Explorers Club flag.

summer of 1934, and included tales drawn from true-to-life Asian adventures, with characters roughly modeled on British/American intelligence operatives he had known in Shanghai. His early Westerns were similarly peppered with details drawn from personal experience. Although therein lay a first hard lesson from the often cruel world of the pulps. His first Westerns were soundly rejected as lacking the authenticity of a Max Brand yarn (a particularly frustrating comment given L. Ron Hubbard's Westerns came straight from his Montana homeland, while Max Brand was a mediocre New York poet named Frederick Schiller Faust, who turned out implausible six-shooter tales from the terrace of an Italian villa).

Nevertheless, and needless to say, L. Ron Hubbard persevered and soon earned a reputation as among the most publishable names in pulp fiction, with a ninety percent placement rate of first-draft manuscripts. He was also among the most prolific, averaging between seventy and a hundred thousand words a month. Hence the rumors that L. Ron Hubbard had redesigned a typewriter for faster keyboard action and pounded out manuscripts on a continuous roll of butcher paper to save the precious seconds it took to insert a single sheet of paper into manual typewriters of the day.

That all L. Ron Hubbard stories did not run beneath said byline is yet another aspect of pulp fiction lore. That is, as publishers periodically rejected manuscripts from top-drawer authors if only to avoid paying top dollar, L. Ron Hubbard and company just as frequently replied with submissions under various pseudonyms. In Ron's case, the

A MAN OF MANY NAMES

Between 1934 and 1950, L. Ron Hubbard authored more than fifteen million words of fiction in more than two hundred classic publications. To supply his fans and editors with stories across an array of genres and pulp titles, he adopted fifteen pseudonyms in addition to his already renowned L. Ron Hubbard byline.

Winchester Remington Colt
Lt. Jonathan Daly
Capt. Charles Gordon
Capt. L. Ron Hubbard
Bernard Hubbel
Michael Keith
Rene Lafayette
Legionnaire 148
Legionnaire 14830
Ken Martin
Scott Morgan
Lt. Scott Morgan
Kurt von Rachen
Barry Randolph
Capt. Humbert Reynolds

list included: Rene Lafayette, Captain Charles Gordon, Lt. Scott Morgan and the notorious Kurt von Rachen—supposedly on the lam for a murder rap, while hammering out two-fisted prose in Argentina. The point: While L. Ron Hubbard as Ken Martin spun stories of Southeast Asian intrigue, LRH as Barry Randolph authored tales of

L. Ron Hubbard, circa 1930, at the outset of a literary career that would finally span half a century.

romance on the Western range—which, stretching between a dozen genres is how he came to stand among the two hundred elite authors providing close to a million tales through the glory days of American Pulp Fiction.

In evidence of exactly that, by 1936 L. Ron Hubbard was literally leading pulp fiction's elite as president of New York's American Fiction Guild. Members included a veritable pulp hall of fame: Lester "Doc Savage" Dent, Walter "The Shadow" Gibson, and the legendary Dashiell Hammett—to cite but a few.

Also in evidence of just where L. Ron Hubbard stood within his first two years on the American pulp circuit: By the spring of 1937, he was ensconced in Hollywood, adopting a Caribbean thriller for Columbia Pictures, remembered today as *The Secret of Treasure Island*. Comprising fifteen thirty-minute episodes, the L. Ron Hubbard screenplay led to the most profitable matinée serial in Hollywood history. In accord with Hollywood culture, he was thereafter continually called upon

The 1937 Secret of Treasure Island, *a fifteen-episode serial adapted for the screen by L. Ron Hubbard from his novel,* Murder at Pirate Castle.

to rewrite/doctor scripts—most famously for long-time friend and fellow adventurer Clark Gable.

In the interim—and herein lies another distinctive chapter of the L. Ron Hubbard story—he continually worked to open Pulp Kingdom gates to up-and-coming authors. Or, for that matter, anyone who wished to write. It was a fairly unconventional stance, as markets were already thin and competition razor sharp. But the fact remains, it was an L. Ron Hubbard hallmark that he vehemently lobbied on behalf of young authors—regularly supplying instructional articles to trade journals, guest-lecturing to short story classes at George Washington University and Harvard, and even founding his own creative writing competition. It was established in 1940, dubbed the Golden Pen, and guaranteed winners both New York representation and publication in *Argosy*.

But it was John W. Campbell Jr.'s *Astounding Science Fiction* that finally proved the most memorable LRH vehicle. While every fan of L. Ron Hubbard's galactic epics undoubtedly knows the story, it nonetheless bears repeating: By late 1938, the pulp publishing magnate of Street & Smith was determined to revamp *Astounding Science Fiction* for broader readership. In particular, senior editorial director F. Orlin Tremaine called for stories with a stronger *human element*. When acting editor John W. Campbell balked, preferring his spaceship-driven tales, Tremaine enlisted Hubbard. Hubbard, in turn, replied with the genre's first truly *character-driven* works, wherein heroes are pitted not against bug-eyed monsters but the mystery and majesty of deep space itself—and thus was launched the Golden Age of Science Fiction.

The names alone are enough to quicken the pulse of any science fiction aficionado, including LRH friend and protégé, Robert Heinlein, Isaac Asimov, A. E. van Vogt and Ray Bradbury. Moreover, when coupled with LRH stories of fantasy, we further come to what's rightly been described as the foundation of every modern tale of horror: L. Ron Hubbard's immortal *Fear.* It was rightly proclaimed by Stephen King as one of the very few works to genuinely warrant that overworked term "classic"—as in: *"This is a classic tale of creeping, surreal menace and horror. . . . This is one of the really, really good ones."*

To accommodate the greater body of L. Ron Hubbard fantasies, Street & Smith inaugurated *Unknown*—a classic pulp if there ever was one, and wherein readers were soon thrilling to the likes of *Typewriter in the Sky* and *Slaves of Sleep* of which Frederik Pohl would declare: *"There are bits and pieces from Ron's work that became part of the language in ways that very few other writers managed."*

L. Ron Hubbard, 1948, among fellow science fiction luminaries at the World Science Fiction Convention in Toronto.

And, indeed, at J. W. Campbell Jr.'s insistence, Ron was regularly drawing on themes from the Arabian Nights and so introducing readers to a world of genies, jinn, Aladdin and Sinbad—all of which, of course, continue to float through cultural mythology to this day.

At least as influential in terms of post-apocalypse stories was L. Ron Hubbard's 1940 *Final Blackout*. Generally acclaimed as the finest anti-war novel of the decade and among the ten best works of the genre ever authored—here, too, was a tale that would live on in ways few other writers imagined.

Portland, Oregon, 1943; L. Ron Hubbard, captain of the US Navy subchaser PC 815.

Hence, the later Robert Heinlein verdict: "Final Blackout *is as perfect a piece of science fiction as has ever been written.*"

Like many another who both lived and wrote American pulp adventure, the war proved a tragic end to Ron's sojourn in the pulps. He served with distinction in four theaters and was highly decorated for commanding corvettes in the North Pacific. He was also grievously wounded in combat, lost many a close friend and colleague and thus resolved to say farewell to pulp fiction and devote himself to what it had supported these many years—namely, his serious research.

But in no way was the LRH literary saga at an end, for as he wrote some thirty years later, in 1980:

"Recently there came a period when I had little to do. This was novel in a life so crammed with busy years, and I decided to amuse myself by writing a novel that was pure *science fiction.*"

That work was *Battlefield Earth: A Saga of the Year 3000*. It was an immediate *New York Times* bestseller and, in fact, the first international science fiction blockbuster in decades. It was not, however, L. Ron Hubbard's magnum opus, as that distinction is generally reserved for his next and final work: The 1.2 million word *Mission Earth*.

> **Final Blackout**
> *is as perfect a piece of science fiction as has ever been written.*
>
> —Robert Heinlein

How he managed those 1.2 million words in just over twelve months is yet another piece of the L. Ron Hubbard legend. But the fact remains, he did indeed author a ten-volume *dekalogy* that lives in publishing history for the fact that each and every volume of the series was also a *New York Times* bestseller.

Moreover, as subsequent generations discovered L. Ron Hubbard through republished works and novelizations of his screenplays, the mere fact of his name on a cover signaled an international bestseller. . . . Until, to date, sales of his works exceed hundreds of millions, and he otherwise remains among the most enduring and widely read authors in literary history. Although as a final word on the tales of L. Ron Hubbard, perhaps it's enough to simply reiterate what editors told readers in the glory days of American Pulp Fiction:

He writes the way he does, brothers, because he's been there, seen it and done it!

THE STORIES FROM THE GOLDEN AGE

Your ticket to adventure starts here with the Stories from the Golden Age collection by master storyteller L. Ron Hubbard. These gripping tales are set in a kaleidoscope of exotic locales and brim with fascinating characters, including some of the most vile villains, dangerous dames and brazen heroes you'll ever get to meet.

The entire collection of over one hundred and fifty stories is being released in a series of eighty books and audiobooks. For an up-to-date listing of available titles, go to www.goldenagestories.com.

AIR ADVENTURE

FAR-FLUNG ADVENTURE

SEA ADVENTURE

TALES FROM THE ORIENT

The Devil—With Wings   *Pearl Pirate*
The Falcon Killer   *The Red Dragon*
Five Mex for a Million   *Spy Killer*
Golden Hell   *Tah*
The Green God   *The Trail of the Red Diamonds*
Hurricane's Roar   *Wind-Gone-Mad*
Inky Odds   *Yellow Loot*
Orders Is Orders

MYSTERY

The Blow Torch Murder   *The Grease Spot*
Brass Keys to Murder   *Killer Ape*
Calling Squad Cars!   *Killer's Law*
The Carnival of Death   *The Mad Dog Murder*
The Chee-Chalker   *Mouthpiece*
Dead Men Kill   *Murder Afloat*
The Death Flyer   *The Slickers*
Flame City   *They Killed Him Dead*

FANTASY

SCIENCE FICTION

WESTERN

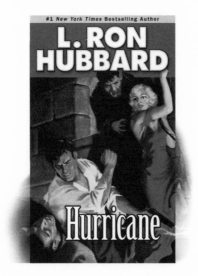

JOIN THE PULP REVIVAL
America in the 1930s and 40s

Pulp fiction was in its heyday and 30 million readers were regularly riveted by the larger-than-life tales of master storyteller L. Ron Hubbard. For this was pulp fiction's golden age, when the writing was raw and every page packed a walloping punch.

That magic can now be yours. An evocative world of nefarious villains, exotic intrigues, courageous heroes and heroines—a world that today's cinema has barely tapped for tales of adventure and swashbucklers.

Enroll today in the Stories from the Golden Age Club and begin receiving your monthly feature edition selected from more than 150 stories in the collection.

You may choose to enjoy them as either a paperback or audiobook for the special membership price of $9.95 each month along with FREE shipping and handling.

CALL TOLL-FREE: **1-877-8GALAXY**
(1-877-842-5299) OR GO ONLINE TO
www.goldenagestories.com
AND BECOME PART OF THE PULP REVIVAL!

Prices are set in US dollars only. For non-US residents, please call
1-323-466-7815 for pricing information. Free shipping available for US residents only.

Galaxy Press, 7051 Hollywood Blvd., Suite 200, Hollywood, CA 90028